Off the _age

Teacher's Resource Module

Lynn Bryan
Charolette Player

CONSULTANTS

Ron Benson

Susan Elliott

Diane Lomond

Ken MacInnis

Kim Newlove

Liz Stenson

GENERAL EDITOR

Kathleen Doyle

Prentice Hall Ginn Canada
Scarborough, Ontario

Canadian Cataloguing in Publication Data

Bryan, Lynn, 1942-
Off the Page. Teacher's resource module

(Collections 6)
ISBN 0-13-010340-3 Atlantic Edition
ISBN 0-13-010351-9 Ontario Edition
ISBN 0-13-010352-7 Western Edition

1. English language – Study and teaching (Elementary). 2.
Language arts (Elementary). I. Player, Charolette. II. Title. III.
Series: Collections (Scarborough, Ont.).

PE1121. O33 1997 Suppl.   428.6   C96-93257-3

Prentice-Hall, Inc., Upper Saddle River, New Jersey
Prentice-Hall International, Inc., London
Prentice-Hall of Australia, Pty., Sydney
Prentice-Hall of India Pvt., Ltd., New Delhi
Prentice-Hall of Japan, Inc., Tokyo
Prentice-Hall of Southeast Asia (PTE) Ltd., Singapore
Editora Prentice-Hall do Brasil Ltda., Rio de Janeiro
Prentice-Hall Hispanoamericana, S.A., Mexico

ISBN 0-13-010340-3 Atlantic Edition
ISBN 0-13-010351-9 Ontario Edition
ISBN 0-13-010352-7 Western Edition
Publisher: Kathleen Doyle
Managing Editor: Carol Stokes
Content Editor: Janis Barr
Copy/Production Editors: Norma Kennedy; Debbie Davies
Editorial Assistant: Caron MacMenamin
Production Co-ordinator: Stephanie Cox
Permissions: Karen Becker
Design: Word & Image Design Studio Inc.
Composition: Brian Lehen • Graphic Design Ltd.
Illustrations: pp. 81, 105; BLMs 16, 20, 21: Vesna Krstanovich

Printed and bound in Canada by Best Book Manufacturers
1 2 3 4 5 6 BBM 03 02 01 2000 99 98

CREDITS

Covers pp. 1, 4, 129, 130, 133, 136, 139: *Whale Brother*, copyright
© 1988. Published by Walker Publishing Company, Inc. Cover art by
Gretchen Will Mayo.
Kids Rule the Internet: The Ultimate Guide, copyright © 1996. Published
by Bloomsbury Children's Books. Cover art by Paul Daviz.
Journey, copyright © 1991. Published by Bantam Doubleday Dell
Books for Young Readers, a Division of Bantam Doubleday Dell
Publishing Group, Inc. Cover art by Barry Moser.
Coast to Coast, copyright © 1992. Published by Bantam Doubleday
Dell Books for Young Readers, a Division of Bantam Doubleday Dell
Publishing Group, Inc.
BLM 5: Excerpt from *Carving a Totem Pole*, copyright © Vickie Jensen,
1994. Published by Douglas & McIntyre Ltd.
BLM 5: Adapted excerpt from "Dancing Bees" by Margery Facklam.
Appeared in SPIDER Magazine, July 1995.
BLM 16: "Up a Rope" from *Mime: A Playbook of Silent Fantasy* by Kay
Hamblin.
BLM 17: Excerpt from *The Last Dragon*, copyright © Susan Miho
Nunes. Published by Clarion Books - a Houghton Mifflin Company
imprint, 1995.

Sources for resources on page 5

Links to Media
- Jeflyn Media Consultants. P.O. Box 220, Mount Albert, ON,
  L0G 1M0. 905-642-6142; Fax: 905-473-1408; 1-800-668-6065
- McIntyre Media. 30 Kelfield Street. Rexdale, ON, M9W 5A2.
  416-245-7800; Fax: 416-245-8600; 1-800-565-3036
- National Film Board. Atlantic Canada: 1-800-561-7104; Quebec:
  1-800-363-0328; Ontario: 1-800-267-7710; Western and
  Northern Canada: 1-800-661-9867
- National Geographic Society. 211 Watline Ave., Ste. 210,
  Mississauga, ON, L4Z 1P3. 905-890-1111; Fax: 905-890-5080;
  1-800-268-2948
- School Services of Canada. 66 Portland St., Toronto, ON,
  M5V 2M8; 416-703-0900; Fax: 416-703-0901; 1-800-387-2084

Links to the Information Highway
- The CD-ROM Shop, 204 Ontario Street, Toronto, ON., M5A 2V5;
  1-800-999-9756; 416-368-5000; Fax: 416-366-9008
  Distribute: *Creative Writer 2; Encarta; Encarta World Atlas;
  Eyewitness Encyclopedia; Multimedia Workshop; Superpaint*
- Core Curriculum Technologies/Software Plus, #1-12760 Bathgate
  Way, Richmond, BC, V6V 1Z4; 1-800-663-7731; Fax: 604-273-6534
  Distribute: *Adventure Canada; Alexander Graham Bell; Canadian
  Encyclopedia; Creative Writer 2; Encarta; Encarta World Atlas;
  Eyewitness Encyclopedia; Multimedia Workshop; Science in
  Your Ear; Superpaint; Totem Poles*
- Educational Resources, 38 Scott St. West, St. Catharines, ON,
  L2R 1C9 Canada: 1-800-565-5198; Ontario: 905-988-3577;
  Fax: 1-800-311-4600
  Distribute: *Canadian Encyclopedia; Creative Writer 2; Encarta;
  Encarta World Atlas; Eyewitness Encyclopedia; Multimedia
  Workshop; Superpaint*
- Educator's Choice Software Company, 29 Meadowview Drive,
  Bedford, NS, B4A 2C3; 902-452-6313; Fax: 902-832-0167
  Distribute: *Adventure Canada; Alexander Graham Bell; Canadian
  Encyclopedia; Creative Writer 2; Encarta; Encarta World Atlas;
  Eyewitness Encyclopedia; Multimedia Workshop; Science in
  Your Ear; Superpaint* (Will take orders for any title.)
- Fitzgerald Studio, 423 Charlotte Street, P. O. Box 963, Sydney,
  NS, B1P 6J4
  Distribute: *Alexander Graham Bell*
- Microsoft Canada, 320 Matheson Blvd. West, Mississauga, ON;
  1-800-933-4750
  Distribute: *Creative Writer 2; Encarta; Encarta World Atlas*

ACKNOWLEDGEMENTS

Prentice Hall Ginn Canada wishes to express its sincere apprecia-
tion to the following Canadian educators for contributing their time
and expertise during the development of this teacher's resource
module.
Kathryn D'Angelo, Vice-Principal, Tomsett Elementary School,
Richmond, BC
Linda Graves, Vice-Principal, Lester B. Pearson Centennial School,
Saskatoon, SK
John O'Brien, Teacher, St. Richard School, Mississauga, ON
Lori Rog, Language Arts Consultant, Regina Public Schools, Regina, SK
Rob Whitworth, Teacher, Beddington Heights Public School, Calgary, AB

Links to the Information Highway, page 5:
Debbie Miller, Teacher, École Van Walleghem School, Winnipeg, MB

Prentice Hall Canada would also like to express its appreciation to
the staff and students of Warden Avenue Junior Public School,
Scarborough, Ontario, and St. Cosmos & Damian School, Toronto,
Ontario, for their assistance with this publication.

Contents

About the Unit

The selections and learning opportunities in this thematic unit focus on the many ways people communicate in ways other than with "pencil and paper"—through the arts, mass media, and personally to others.

UNIT FOCUS

This unit will help students develop concepts pertaining to
- communicating/expressing yourself through **the arts**
- communicating through **mass media**
- communicating **in person**

Throughout the unit, students will have many opportunities to
- make connections between the relationships and special activities presented in the literature in *Off the Page* and those they experience with their own lives

- use language for many purposes, most notably to
  - recount and narrate experiences
  - describe feelings, thoughts, and responses
  - reveal something about themselves
  - relate to others and their experiences
  - explore forms of the arts and mass media
  - gather and organize information

LANGUAGE ARTS LEARNING EXPECTATIONS

As students participate in the learning experiences in the *Off the Page* unit, they will meet expectations pertaining to the following:

Reading

Students will
- read a variety of fiction and non-fiction materials for different purposes—poetry, biography, procedural text, photos/commentary, picture book story, photo essay
- read independently, selecting appropriate reading strategies
- explain their interpretation of a written work, supporting it with evidence from the work and from their own knowledge and experience
- identify a writer's perspective or character's motivation
- identify different forms of writing and describe their characteristics

Writing

Students will
- communicate ideas and information for a variety of purposes and to specific audiences— message, commentary, image phrases, interview
- use writing for various purposes and in a range of contexts
- use a variety of sentence types
- use correctly the conventions—spelling, grammar, punctuation
- select words and expressions to create specific effects

Oral Communication

Students will
- communicate a main idea about a topic and describe a sequence of events
- use tone of voice and gestures to enhance the message and help convince or persuade listeners in conversations, discussions, or presentations
- follow up on others' ideas, and recognize the validity of different points of view in group discussions or problem-solving activities

Visual Communication

Students will
- analyze and assess a media work and express a considered viewpoint about it
- create a variety of media works—model, picture, photography, flow diagram, mime

(See *Appendix 1* for specific indicators of each expectation.)

Unit Resources

Student Books

ANTHOLOGY

The *Off the Page* **anthology** contains a range of fiction and non-fiction selections of both published and student writing. It is intended for instructional use in a whole class or group teaching/learning context.

GENRE BOOKS AND NOVELS

There are two **genre books** and two **novels** to provide sustained reading of longer prose pieces. They can be used in small group literature circles for book and novel study.

GENRE BOOKS

• *Whale Brother,* by Barbara Steiner. This picture book tells how Omu wants to become a great carver of ivory like Padloq. But Padloq tells him that he must first find the qarrtsiluni, the stillness. An adventure with his whale brothers shows Omu what he needs to know.

• *Kids Rule the Internet,* by Jason Page. This guide to the Internet and the World Wide Web will help kids (and adults!) learn how to get around, and to navigate the Information Highway.

NOVELS

• *Journey,* by Patricia MacLachlan. Journey, saddened and angered by his mother's sudden departure, spends his summer trying to understand why she left him and his sister with their grandparents. With the help of a camera, a cat, and shutterbug Grandpa, Journey finds his past and, more importantly, his present.

• *Coast to Coast,* by Betsy Byars. Birch decides that the best thing for both her and her grandfather would be a coast-to-coast flight across America in Grandpa's antique Piper Cub. Along the way, they both begin to come to terms with their pasts, and find some answers, though not the sort they expected.

Strategies for using the genre books and novels can be found on pages 129-142 of this guide and in the book *Teaching with Novels, Books, and Poetry.*

Teacher Materials

The **Teacher's Resource Module** for *Off the Page* presents teaching and assessment activities for each of the selections in the student book.

The **blackline masters** intended for use with this unit are included at the back of the Teacher's Resource Module. The blackline masters include masters that are additional activities and home link masters.

Learning Strategy Cards introduced in this unit are

39. Purposes of Language

40. Parts of Speech

41. Apostrophes

42. Taking Photographs

43. Using a Search Engine

44. Writing an Introductory Paragraph

45. Self-Evaluation

46. Speeches

47. Interviewing

48. Learning to Memorize

49. Writing Dialogue

50. Types of Sentences

These cards are available within the **COLLECTIONS 6 Teacher's Resources** as a pack of 62 cards. Templates for some cards are available on disk (compatible with Mac and IBM).

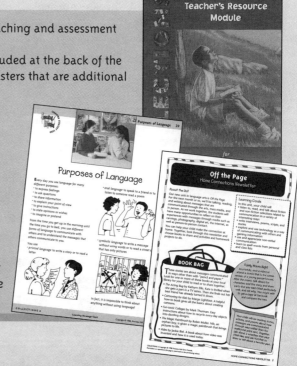

Read-Aloud Books

Choose a book to read aloud throughout this unit.
- Booth, David (compiler) *Images of Nature: Canadian Poets and the Group of Seven*. Toronto: Kids Can Press, 1995. 32 pp.
- Cunningham Julia. *Burnish Me Bright*. New York: Pantheon, 1970.
- Feiffer, Jules. *The Man in the Ceiling*. New York: HarperCollins, 1994. 185 pp.
- O'Neal, Zibby. *In Summer Light*. New York: Viking Kestrel, 1985. 160 pp.
- Paterson, Katherine. *Jacob Have I Loved*. New York: HarperCollins, 1990. 256 pp.
- Voight, Cynthia. *Dicey's Song*. New York: Fawcett, 1987. 211 pp.
- Yep, Laurence. *The Ink-Keeper's Apprentice*. New York: Puffin, 1996. 160 pp.

Personal Reading

With help from the school librarian and the students, assemble a classroom library of books pertaining to the unit for students to browse through and choose for personal reading. The following books are suggested:
- Ahmad, Nyla. *Cybersurfer*. Toronto: Owl Books, 1995. 71 pp. Non-fiction. Cdn. Average reading level.
- Brown, Susan, and Anne Stephenson. *The Mad Hacker*. Richmond Hill, ON: Scholastic Canada, 1987. 113 pp. Novel. Cdn. Average reading level.
- Brust, Beth Wagner. *The Amazing Paper Cuttings of Hans Christian Andersen*. New York: Ticknor & Fields, 1994. 80 pp. Non-fiction. Average reading level.
- Cooper, Susan. *The Boggart*. New York: Simon & Schuster, 1993. 208 pp. Novel. Average reading level.
- Gosse, Bonnie. *Soapstone Carving for Children*. Waterloo: Penumbra Press, 1991. Non-fiction. Cdn. Average reading level.
- Jenkins, Patrick. *Flipbook Animation: And Other Ways to Make Cartoons Move*. Toronto: Kids Can Press, 1991. 96 pp. Non-fiction. Cdn. Average reading level.
- Lawson, Julie. *Cougar Cove*. Victoria: Orca, 1996. 138 pp. Novel. Cdn. Easy to average reading level.
- Lind, Jane. *Gathie Falk*. Vancouver: Douglas & McIntyre, 1989. 40 pp. Biography. Cdn. Average reading level.
- MacLeod, Elizabeth. *The Phone Book: Instant Communication from Smoke Signals to Satellites and Beyond*. Toronto: Kids Can Press, 1995. 64 pp. Non-fiction. Cdn. Average reading level.
- Shaw-MacKinnon, Margaret. *Tiktala*. Toronto: Stoddart, 1996. 32 pp. Picture book. Cdn. Easy to average reading level.
- Wallace, Shelagh. *The TV Book: The Kids' Guide to Talking Back*. Toronto: Annick Press, 1996. 96 pp. Non-ficton. Cdn. Average reading level.
- Woolaver, Lance. *The Metallic Sparrow*. Halifax: Nimbus Publishing, 1992. 126 pp. Novel. Cdn. Average reading level.

Links to Media

These videos relate to topics within the unit.
- *Body Language: An Introduction to Non-Verbal Communication*. McIntyre Media, 1994. 25 min.
- *Drawing a Blank*. International Tele-Film, 1996. 30 min.
- *Live TV*. National Film Board, 1996. 22 min.
- *The Mystery of the Cave Paintings*. International Tele-Film, 1996. 16 min.
- *The Story African Masks Tell*. School Services of Canada, 1993. 22 min
- *Video Pen Pals: Hong Kong*. Jeflyn Media, 1996. 15 min.

Links to the Information Highway

Software such as that listed below can be used to extend learning on the topic or on selected learning outcomes of the unit.
- *Adventure Canada* from VR Didatech Software: Explore Canada through slides, videos, text, and graphics. *Win/Mac CD-ROM*
- *The 1997 Canadian Encyclopedia Plus* from McClelland & Stewart: A current Canadian reference includes thousands of illustrations, Quicktime movies, animation, sound clips, and over 600 maps. *Mac/Win 3.1 CD-ROM*
- *Creative Writer 2* from Microsoft: A program of writing and drawing tools. *Win 3.1/Win 95, CD-ROM*
- *Encarta* from Microsoft: This multimedia encyclopedia integrates with the user's word processor, allowing text, images, and sound to be incorporated in reports and other documents. Offers world wide web links. *Win/Mac CD-ROM*
- *Encarta World Atlas* from Microsoft: Culture articles examine people, lifestyles, and societies of all countries. Detailed printed maps, thousands of multimedia images and photographs from around the world. *Win '95 CD-ROM*
- *Eyewitness Encyclopedia of Science* by Dorling Kindersley: Interactive exploration of science links common principles of science and technology, applies them to everyday life. *Mac/Win CD-ROM*
- *The Multimedia Workshop* by Davidson: Three workshops— a writing workshop, a video workshop, and a paint workshop—allow students to create printed documents and video presentations. *Mac/Win CD-ROM*
- *Science in Your Ear* from MECC: Hands-on experiments and simulations done both on and off screen, using students' own voices, ears, and musical instruments. *Mac/Win CD-ROM*
- *SuperPaint 3.5 Deluxe* from Adobe: Combines the best of painting and drawing features in an easy to use graphics program. *Mac CD-ROM*
- *Totem Poles* from VR Didatech Software: Elaborates on the varied styles and meanings of totem pole traditions found along the northwest coast. Over 200 poles and their stories; interviews with carvers; pole-raising ceremonies. *Mac/Win CD-ROM*

Note: Sources for these videos and software products are listed with the credits on page (ii).

UNIT OVERVIEW

Topic Focus	OFF THE PAGE Anthology ♣ = Canadian 🎧 = available on audio (student writing is indented)	Genre	Reading Level Range				COLLECTIONS 6 Genre Book Links
			4	5	6	7	
COMMUNI-CATING/ EXPRESSING YOURSELF THROUGH THE ARTS	How Music Was Fetched Out of Heaven	myth retold			•		
	🎧 Creators	poems					
	A Young Painter: The Life and Paintings of Wang Yani	biography				•	*Whale Brother* by Barbara Steiner
	🎧 ♣ Carving a Totem Pole	procedural text		•			
	♣ Wildland Visions	photos/commentary			•		
	🎧 ♣ A Musical Note	personal narrative					4 5 6 7
	🎧 ♣ Painting	essay					(box at 6)
	🎧 ♣ Music in My Life	personal narrative					
COMMUNI-CATING THROUGH MASS MEDIA	♣ Get Set for the Net!	non-fiction account			•		
	♣ Fast Forward Art	computer art with commentaries		•			*Kids Rule the Internet: The Ultimate Guide* by Jason Page
	♣ World Shrinkers	article			•		
	Fax Facts	short story			•		4 5 6 7
	♣ In Your Face	photo essay			•		(box at 7)
	🎧 ♣ Meet Emily of New Moon	interview			•		
	♣ Fax Facts	limerick					
	♣ Ways to Communicate	acrostic poem					
	♣ Log On	short story					
	♣ Conflict Resolution	e-mail messages					
	♣ My Hobby	personal narrative					
COMMUNI-CATING IN PERSON	🎧 Anti-Snore Machine	short story			•		
	🎧 ♣ Listen with Your Eyes	article			•		
	🎧 Dancing the Cotton-Eyed Joe	short story			•		
	All the Places to Love	picture book story			•		
	Speak Your Dreams	poems					
	♣ The Smile	poem					
	♣ Sign Language	report					

Criteria for Reading Level Range

Key: The Reading Level Range is the independent level. The solid boxes indicate the overall readability. The dot indicates the range.

Factors that we considered:
- *concept load*: number and nature of new concepts, amount of exemplification, contextual support
- *language considerations*: vocabulary, sentence patterns, and complexity
- *writing style and tone*: familiar or unfamiliar, informal or formal
- *genre type and structure*: familiarity, predictability, and repetitiveness of the elements of the story or writing form
- *selection length*
- *classroom reality*: selections represent a range of abilities in a Grade 6 classroom

Factors that you may also consider:
- *familiarity*: each student's background knowledge and familiarity with the topic
- *student interest*: each student's degree of interest in and motivation for the topic and/or content of the selection
- *reading stage/level of the student*: whether he/she can read it independently,

COLLECTIONS 6 Novel Links	Other COLLECTIONS 6 Anthology Links	Other PRENTICE HALL GINN Links
Journey by Patricia MacLachlan 4 5 6 7	The Flute Player (Unit 5) *short story* Market! (Unit 5) *paintings/commentary*	Spotlight: The Famous People Players (RW) Exploring Mime (S6) A World of Imagination (L9) Behind the Scenes (L9)
	Saturn: Lord of the Rings (Unit 3) *article* Seeing Stars (Unit 3) *photo essay*	The Making of Green Gables (RW) Jingle Jangle (RW) The Justine Blainey Story (RW) Television Drama (L9)
Coast to Coast by Betsy Byars 4 5 6 7	I Want to Be (Unit 1) *prose poem* Now That's Olympic History (Unit 5) *article* The Olympics/Sports (Unit 5) *student writing* The Elders Are Watching (Unit 5) poem	Fortune's Friend (L10) The Gift of Grace (RW) The Origin of Stories (S6)

with teacher guidance, with peer support, or in a listen-and-read approach only
- *reading strategy used*: the reading strategies suggested in the *Teacher's Resource Module* are intended to allow most Grade 6 students to enjoy and understand the selections
- *language level of the student*: whether or not the student's birth language is English

Keys:

The *COLLECTIONS* 6 units referred to in the second last column are as follows:

Unit 1: *Looking for Answers*
Unit 2: *Tales—Heroes, Deeds, and Wonders*
Unit 3: *Space, Stars, and Quasars*
Unit 5: *Discovering Links*

Letter codes in the last column indicate the following Prentice Hall Ginn publications:
S6 = *Journeys: Springboards 6*
RW = *Journeys: Ride the Wave*
L9 = *Literacy 2000*: Stage 9
L10 = *Literacy 2000*: Stage 10

ONGOING LEARNING OPPORTUNITIES

The following activities can be initiated over two to three days to
- launch student interest in the unit.
- provide a common base for class, group, or individual learning experiences.
- engage the students in sustained learning throughout the unit.
- establish a procedure for spelling workshops.

Read aloud a book

Choose one or more of the books on page 5 to read aloud to the class throughout the unit study.

Establish a writing area

Create an environment that supports process writing. Explain to the students that they can use this area to write about topics they are interested in, to discuss their writing with you or one another, to keep their writing portfolios, and to consult reference sources.

Involve the students in preparing the writing area by gathering the necessary writing materials and setting out dictionaries, thesauri, and Learning Strategy Cards related to writing. They can display models and/or charts of different types of writing, along with vocabulary charts, such as lists of synonyms and descriptive words.

They might also include any tips for writing provided in the profiles after the main anthology selections and on the student writing pages. Students can continue to add to their charts as they encounter new ideas and advice in other units or as they develop their own ideas.

Set up a unit bulletin board

An ongoing bulletin board display could feature pictures and information related to topics in the selections, as well as the students' writing and other pieces of work they create throughout the unit. The unit title, *Off the Page*, can be an overall heading for the bulletin board, with more specific headings being made from time to time for particular groupings of work displayed. Some specific suggestions for displays are provided in the teaching plans for the selections.

Consider having a small group of students be facilitators for creating the display. This group would be responsible for such things as gathering their peers' work, arranging the pieces on the bulletin board in an organized and connected way, creating headings, and changing the display at an appropriate time.

Use computers

Using available equipment and space, set up a computer learning centre. Perhaps establish a sign-up timetable to allow students to best plan their time at this centre. Allow students to choose from a variety of activities appropriate to their abilities and needs. Using the computer, students can write and illustrate personal stories and memories, journals, mini-books, fold-out books, personal dictionaries, or spelling lists. Some can be put on display and others taken home to be shared with family and relatives. Books they write can be loaned to the school library or another classroom. Included in the computer centre can be a variety of software related to the theme, including the CD-ROM component of this program.

Look for this symbol throughout the unit to find links to computers, other electronic media, and technical writing.

Link to the home

To reinforce learning between the home and the school,
- use the *Home Connections Newsletter,* Blackline Masters 1-2, sending these pages home at appropriate times during the unit.
- encourage students to bring resources from home such as books, magazines, video cassettes, computer games that pertain to communication through the arts, through mass media, or in person.
- invite students to share favorite stories or poems they have read or written throughout the unit with their families, caregivers, and friends.
- look for the home link symbol  throughout the unit.

Plan for spelling workshops

Spelling strategies and activities are provided in eight selected teaching plans in the *Off the Page* unit. In this unit and subsequent units of *COLLECTIONS,* the focus is to integrate spelling.

Teachers can
- choose a few **high utility words** to focus on each week, perhaps in collaboration with students. Refer to high utility lists compiled by such people as Ves Thomas, Mary Tarasoff, Rebecca Sitton, or Edward Fry.
- have students select some **personal words** they would like to learn to spell. They can draw these words from various subject areas, difficult words encountered in personal writing, words related to the theme, or other words that interest them. In their personal dictionaries, students may record these words, their meanings, synonyms, antonyms, pronunciation, and so on. Learning Strategy Card 1, *Using a Thesaurus,* can be used to help students who wish to look up and record synonyms.
- use or adapt the **unit spelling words** compiled from the prose selections. These words highlight particular patterns, structures and strategies, and include early level and challenge lists. (See Appendix 3, page 178, for an overview of unit spelling words.)
- use the spelling **blackline masters** provided with the selections to produce word cards for sorting and study. (See *Language Workshop — Spelling*, page 17 of this guide.)

For each group of spelling words, there are specific activities in the *Language Workshop — Spelling* section of the selection teaching plan.

How Music Was Fetched Out of Heaven

In this Mexican myth, retold by Geraldine McCaughrean, Quetzalcoatl outsmarts the Sun and causes music to come to Earth. This ends the silence that both the Earth and its people have suffered.

Anthology, pages 4–7

Blackline Master 23

Learning Strategy Card 39

Learning Choices

LINK TO EXPERIENCE

Discuss the Need for Music

Recall "How" Tales and Myths

READ AND RESPOND TO TEXT

READING FOCUS
- identify the elements of a story and explain how they relate to each other
- STRATEGY: **double look**

REVISIT THE TEXT

READING
Classify Images
- read a variety of fiction and non-fiction materials for different purposes

WRITING
Write a Message
- produce pieces of writing using a variety of forms, techniques, and resources appropriate to the form and purpose, and materials from other media
Language Workshop — Spelling
- ous pattern; suffixes; irregular spellings

ORAL COMMUNICATION
Choose Background Music
- analyze and assess a media work and express a considered viewpoint about it

LINK TO CURRICULUM

LANGUAGE ARTS
Write a "How" Story

SCIENCE
Find Out About Sound Waves

Research Alexander Graham Bell

ART
Create a Picture Story

SOCIAL STUDIES
Make an Ancient Mayan Question-and-Answer Book

Key Learning Expectations

Students will
- identify the elements of a story and explain how they relate to each other (**Reading Focus, p. 11**)
- read a variety of fiction and non-fiction materials for different purposes (**Reading Mini Lesson, p. 12**)
- produce pieces of writing using a variety of forms, techniques, and resources appropriate to the form and purpose, and materials from other media (**Writing Mini Lesson, p. 12**)
- analyze and assess a media work and express a considered viewpoint about it (**Oral Communication Mini Lesson, p. 14**)

LINK TO EXPERIENCE

Discuss the Need for Music

Ask the students to imagine that they live in a world where there is no music in their lives—no bands or symphonies, no singing, no whistling. Arrange them in small groups to discuss and share their opinions about this situation by posing questions such as:
- What would you miss most about not having music in your life?
- Why is having music in our lives important? What does it do for us?
- Can you think of any advantages to not having music as a part of our lives?

Each group could organize the results of their discussion in a yes/no T-chart entitled "Music Is Important in Our Lives." The charts could then be shared with the class.

Recall "How" Tales and Myths

Ask the students to think back on the tales/myths they have read that explain how things came to be and to talk about the unique features of these "how" or pourquoi stories. List their responses; for example:

- explain something about nature, the world
- are set in the past
- were passed on orally long before they were written down
- are part of a culture's history and tradition
- usually contain supernatural or impossible events or happenings
- tales usually have animal characters that act like people
- myths involve gods or goddesses, heroes, or monsters

To extend the activity, the students might like to share their favorite pourquoi stories in small groups.

READ AND RESPOND TO TEXT

Reading Focus

Use a variation of the **double look** strategy. Have the students read the selection through for the first time to gain an understanding of the plot, then invite them to come together in small groups to share and discuss their personal responses to the events of the story, the actions of Quetzalcoatl, and the story's ending.

On the second reading, have the students reread the selection in pairs to summarize the plot by detailing the introduction, the rising action, the climax, the falling action, and the conclusion of the story, using a plot diagram to organize the events. Pairs can then share and compare their diagrams in small groups.

 A sample of a plot diagram can be found on page 23 of the *Program Information Book*.

A sample of a plot diagram can be found on page 23 of the *Program Information Book*.

Reader Response

Students could
- hold a conversation about the story to discuss questions such as:
  - **Do you think Quetzalcoatl is a hero in this story? Why or why not?**
  - **How do you think the Sun would describe Quetzalcoatl?**
  - **How did the world change after music came? Why do you think the music didn't change the Sun in this way?**
  - **What did you like best about this myth? Why?**
- illustrate their favorite part of the myth.
- retell the story to a friend or family member using facial expression and body language to add to the drama of the telling.

Get Ready to Read

Have the students read the title and then with a partner brainstorm ways that they think music could be fetched out of the heavens. Ask them to jot their ideas in a journal or notebook. As they read the story, they could compare their ideas with those presented in the selection.

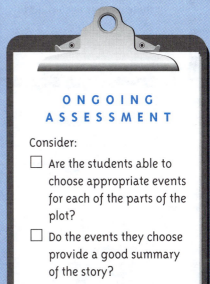

ONGOING ASSESSMENT

Consider:
- ☐ Are the students able to choose appropriate events for each of the parts of the plot?
- ☐ Do the events they choose provide a good summary of the story?

Reading

Classify Images

Talk with the students about the way many authors use imagery (descriptions and figures of speech) that enables readers to create vivid pictures in their minds while reading. Jot some examples of imagery from the story, such as the following, and talk about the pictures they create for the students—what they see, hear, feel, taste, or smell in their minds:

– the groan of the wind ...
– Like hounds, they [the winds] came bounding over the bending treetops.
– This place was too hot for tears, too bright for shadows.

In pairs, have the students revisit the story to find examples of imagery and jot each of their retrieved images on self-stick notes or small pieces of paper. Then, have them arrange the notes into groups on a desk, based on a common criteria of their choosing. For example, "groan of the wind" and "crash of sea" can be grouped together because they describe sounds of nature. Ask them to label each of their groupings with a title that indicates the classification. Emphasize to the students that the images can be grouped in a number of ways, and that there is no right or wrong classification.

Upon completion, encourage the partners to visit each others' desk display of groupings and compare the variety of ways in which classmates chose to organize their examples of images.

Writing

Write a Message

Learning Strategy Card 39

Use Learning Strategy Card 39, *Purposes of Language*, as the basis for a class discussion on the different purposes of language and the different writing forms that can be used for each of these purposes. For example, a letter can give information, describe, or persuade; a story can describe, teach a lesson, or provide a different viewpoint; a poem can describe, persuade, or analyze.

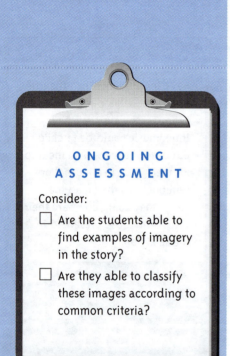

ONGOING ASSESSMENT

Consider:
- ☐ Are the students able to find examples of imagery in the story?
- ☐ Are they able to classify these images according to common criteria?

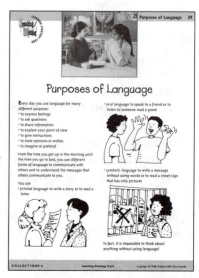

Have the students think back to the selection and the form the author used to share the message that the world needs music and discuss the effectiveness of the choice. Have them brainstorm other forms of writing that could be used to convey this same message. Together, choose one of these and talk about the criteria/characteristics of the form. For example, a friendly letter

• is written to someone close.
• shares personal feelings and experiences.
• is written like a conversation.
• begins with a friendly greeting and ends with a closing comment.

Compose the start of a friendly letter, or the form discussed by the class, that expresses the importance of music to the writer.

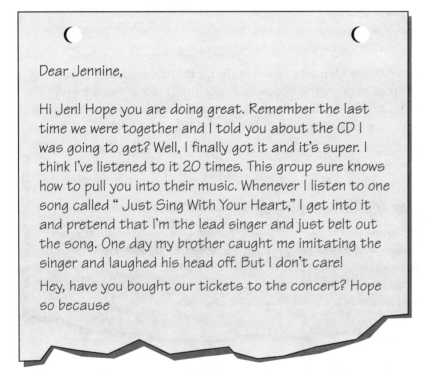

Dear Jennine,

Hi Jen! Hope you are doing great. Remember the last time we were together and I told you about the CD I was going to get? Well, I finally got it and it's super. I think I've listened to it 20 times. This group sure knows how to pull you into their music. Whenever I listen to one song called " Just Sing With Your Heart," I get into it and pretend that I'm the lead singer and just belt out the song. One day my brother caught me imitating the singer and laughed his head off. But I don't care!

Hey, have you bought our tickets to the concert? Hope so because

Throughout this unit, there are several opportunities for the students to write for a variety of purposes, in a variety of forms. It is assumed that the students will engage in a writing process beginning with pre-writing activities that lead them into and through the drafting, revising, and editing stages and, when appropriate, culminating in a polished piece of work that is suitable for presenting or publishing.

Ask the students to choose a form that they feel would get their message of the importance of music across to a reader. Suggest that they think about the criteria for the form before they begin to write.

The students can share their first drafts in small groups and discuss the effectiveness of each form in fulfilling the purpose.

For **Language Workshop — Spelling**, see page 17.

As an activity before this lesson, you may wish to ask the students to listen for the background music in a television program or movie and think about what it adds to the action or mood of the story.

Refer to the rich images and wording found in this selection, and with the students, discuss what effect background music might have if the myth were read aloud. Then read the following excerpt from the selection and ask them to suggest types of background music or specific pieces of music that would best fit the words and their message. List and discuss their suggestions.

He whistled up the winds like hounds. Like hounds they came bounding over the bending treetops, over the red places where dust rose up in twisting columns, and over the sea, whipping the waters into mountainous waves. Baying and howling, they carried Quetzalcoatl higher and higher—higher than all Creation—so high that he could glimpse the Sun ahead of him.

Have the students brainstorm things that would be important to keep in mind when choosing background music for the oral reading of a particular passage or part of a story. Together, draw up some guidelines for choosing and playing background music.

Guidelines for Choosing/Playing Background Music

- decide on the mood of the section— what feeling(s) do you get from the part
- choose background music that gives you the same feelings as the section
- music and words should match and complement each other
- music should not be too loud so reader can be heard
- can play music before section is read to set the mood

Arrange students in groups to select a paragraph or section from the story and find appropriate music to be used as the text is read aloud. Or, they may prefer to choose a part of another story they have read.

 Suggest that the students talk to the music teacher in the school or to family members for help in finding the "right" music.

After each group has practised, they can read aloud their portion of the selection accompanied by the background music to the class.

 See **Assess Learning**, page 16.

LINK TO CURRICULUM

Language Arts

Write a "How" Story

Invite the students to create their own "How" story following the criteria they established in the "Link To Experience" activity. Or, if the activity was not done, develop a list of criteria first with the students. Brainstorm a number of possibilities for "how" stories and list the ideas on chart paper.

Suggest to the students that they explore their chosen "how" topic with a partner to discuss characters, plot, and story theme before they begin to write.

 Students could use a word processing program such as *Creative Writer 2* to embellish the final product of their "How" story. (See pages 5 and (ii) for resource information.)

Science

Find Out About Sound Waves

Interested students could work in a group to investigate sound: what the components of sound are, how it is made, why we can hear it, why different animals can hear different pitches of sound, and so on. They could make a booklet on sound, with diagrams to help explain some of the information. Encourage the students to seek information from a number of sources: reference books, magazines, the Internet, CD-ROMs, and so on.

Research Alexander Graham Bell

Some students may wish to extend their "sound" research to find out about Alexander Graham Bell and his work with sound. They could create a fact sheet outlining important facts about this inventor and his work and display the sheets so other students could compare the facts they gathered with those of their classmates.

 Interested students could access a website called "The Kids Zone" at **http://bell.uccb.ns.ca:80/kids/kidpag.3htm** or they could enter the words **The Kids Zone** into a search engine. The Web page offers complete instructions along with a list of required material and steps to follow, so students can recreate Bell's experiments. The CD-ROM, *Alexander Graham Bell,* also offers a great deal of information about his life and work. (See pages 5 and (ii) for resource information.)

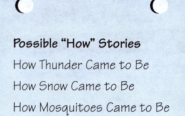

Possible "How" Stories
How Thunder Came to Be
How Snow Came to Be
How Mosquitoes Came to Be
How Hyenas Got Their Laugh

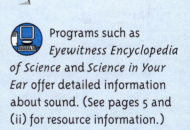

Programs such as *Eyewitness Encyclopedia of Science* and *Science in Your Ear* offer detailed information about sound. (See pages 5 and (ii) for resource information.)

The Arts

Create a Picture Story

Students could retell the main points of this myth, or another favorite myth or tale, through pictures. Suggest that they divide the story into four to six sections and provide an illustration that depicts the main event/idea of each section. They can choose their favorite medium for the illustrations: watercolor, ink etchings, pastels, paper collage, and so on.

Each student could arrange the finished pictures onto a large piece of paper for display. Encourage them to write a brief caption for each picture.

Social Studies

Make an Ancient Mayan Question-and-Answer Book

Groups of students could get together to share what they know about the Ancient Mayan civilization of Mexico and then brainstorm a list of questions they would like answered. Each student in the group could choose one or more questions to research. The results of their research could be organized into a question-and-answer booklet for the classroom or school library.

Assess Learning

Oral Communication (see p. 14)

Choose three students to **peer assess** each read-aloud/ background music presentation, ensuring that all students have the opportunity to participate in an assessment. Use the guidelines established in the lesson to develop a rating scale, with 1 being the lowest and 5 the highest. For example:

Background Music Rating Scale

	1	2	3	4	5
1. Music matched mood of the story	1	2	3	4	5
2. Music was an appropriate volume	1	2	3	4	5
3. Music added to the enjoyment of the reading	1	2	3	4	5
4. Overall impression of the presentation	1	2	3	4	5

Comments: _____
_____
_____

Provide time for the students doing the assessment to share their assessment with the group.

Blackline Master 23

Explore and Discover

Use Blackline Master 23 to make overhead transparency cards and to reproduce copies for students to use.

Review the meaning of some words by composing oral sentences using words students are unsure of. Guide students as they **sort** the word cards. Suggest that they first group the words according to meaning, then into categories of their own choice according to word structure, phonetic patterns, and so on. Invite them to **share** their groupings using the overhead transparency cards.

Discuss the common features and spelling patterns in the words, focusing first on the "ous" and suffix patterns. Have the students suggest other words with the same patterns, or look through their own writing or books they're reading to find other examples. Students can begin ongoing wall **charts,** listing words with selected suffixes and the "ous" pattern. These can be added to throughout the unit.

Note the list words with the "ness" suffix to make students aware that "ness" creates a noun indicating a condition or a state of mind or being.

Have the students find words with irregular spellings. Reinforce the idea that it is important to develop the habit of looking up irregularly spelled words in the dictionary, even if just for confirmation.

Invite the students to identify parts of words that might cause difficulties, and as a group, think of ways to remember the correct spelling.

Pretest

Administer the word list as a pretest, perhaps using the spelling buddy approach. Dictate the words, each time saying the word, using it in a sentence related to "How Music Was Fetched Out of Heaven," and then repeating the word. Collaboratively correct the words. Show each word, asking students to put a dot under the letters they have spelled correctly, and to underline or highlight places where they had errors. Students can list the words they need to study.

Students who have few or no errors could
• study Theme/Challenge Words from the story.
• locate and practise spelling challenging words from their own writing.

HOW MUSIC WAS FETCHED OUT OF HEAVEN

• ous pattern; suffixes; irregular spellings

unfriendliness	contentment	mountainous
fiery	nothingness	generous
dangerously	siege	readiness
column	marvellous	mightiest

Theme/Challenge Words

• music and world of the gods

Quetzalcoatl	Tezcatlipoca	cadence
citadel	monumental	

Early Words

• -le pattern

tremble	grumble	circle
cable	miracle	

• play or create word games.
• act as spelling resource leaders for other students.

Students experiencing difficulty could
• be given fewer or less difficult words.
• study the Early Words and other pattern words related to them.

Study and Practise

Students could
• use Learning Strategy Card 4 to study words identified after the pretest.
• on the front of the word cards, highlight in different colors the suffixes, "ous" pattern, and the tricky part in the irregularly spelled words.
• write the words they misspelled along the shape of a music note, clef, or staff.

Post Test

Administer the post test. For those students who have a modified list, give the test at another time. Record the number of words each student spelled correctly and note the improvement since the pretest. Identify the types of errors the students made and use these for reteaching and study.

SPELLING BUDDIES

Pair students of like abilities and have them be responsible for dictating words for the tests to each other. Spelling buddies can help one another in checking the pretest, and in their study and practise.

Creators

The poems "I am the creativity" by Alexis De Veaux and "The Artist" by Ashley Bryan celebrate the gift of creativity.

Anthology, pages 8-9   Blackline Master 3

Learning Choices

LINK TO EXPERIENCE

Define Creativity

Write About Self-Expression

READ AND RESPOND TO TEXT

READING FOCUS
* explain their interpretation of a written work, supporting it with evidence from the work and from their own knowledge and experience
* STRATEGY: **visualize and sketch**

REVIST THE TEXT

READING
Compare Poems
* read a variety of fiction and non-fiction materials for different purposes

WRITING
Appreciate and Write Metaphors
* select words and expressions to create specific effects (metaphors)

VISUAL COMMUNICATION
Paint a Picture
* create a variety of media works

LINK TO CURRICULUM

LANGUAGE ARTS
Read Poetry

Investigate an Artist

THE ARTS
Present Forms of Self-Expression

Illustrate Metaphors

Key Learning Expectations

Students will
* explain their interpretation of a written work, supporting it with evidence from the work and from their own knowledge and experience (**Reading Focus, p. 19**)
* read a variety of fiction and non-fiction materials for different purposes (**Reading Mini Lesson, p. 19**)
* select words and expressions to create specific effects (metaphors) (**Writing Mini Lesson, p. 20**)
* create a variety of media works (**Visual Communication Mini Lesson, p. 21**)

LINK TO EXPERIENCE

Define Creativity

Together with the students, define the term "creativity" and ask them to share examples of what they think creativity is. List their examples and discuss their perceptions of the term. Following the talk, ask them to complete the following sentence in as many ways as they can.

I am creative when....

Organize the students into conversation circles to share their sentences. Bring the groups together to talk about the similarities and differences in responses.

For suggestions and techniques regarding Conversation Circles, refer to Learning Strategy Card 24.

Write About Self-Expression

Ask the students to think about how they most enjoy expressing their feelings and attitudes about things that are important to them; for example, by writing, painting, drawing, ... Encourage them to write about their most preferred way of self-expression and tell why it is special to them. Provide time for them to share their writing with a partner, if they wish.

READ AND RESPOND TO TEXT

Reading Focus

Use a variation of the listen and visualize strategy, **visualize and sketch.** Read both poems aloud, or play the *COLLECTIONS* audio version of the selection while the students listen. Provide time for the students to quickly sketch the images that come to their minds as they listen to the poems. You may wish to read the poems more than once while the students complete their initial sketches.

Read the poems aloud a second time, while the students follow along. Allow time for them to add to or modify their sketches. The students can then share and discuss their sketches with a partner or a small group, telling why they drew the images they did, and compare their interpretations of the poems to those of the illustrator.

Get Ready to Read

To introduce this selection, read the selection title and the titles of the poems aloud, and ask the students to talk about:
• what the titles make them think about
• what they think the common theme of the poems might be
• what each poem might be about

Reader Response

Students could
• read aloud the poem they liked the best with a partner or group, using their voices expressively.
• write a description of the man in the poem,"The Artist," using information from the poem.
• create three different questions to ask a classmate about these poems.
• use their sketches as the basis for a more detailed drawing, using whatever colors, medium, and drawing style they feel best represents their images.

REVISIT THE TEXT

Reading

Compare Poems

Create a Venn diagram by placing two hoops on the floor so that they overlap, or by drawing two intersecting circles on the chalkboard or on an overhead transparency. Label one ring "The Artist" and the other "I am the creativity."

▶

Ask the students to reread the poems and discuss such things as main message, images created, feelings and attitudes expressed, general tone, and so on of each poem. As each idea is expressed, write it on the board or overhead in the appropriate circle, or on cards that can be placed within the hoops. Any ideas that are applicable for both poems should be written/placed in the intersecting portion of the circles.

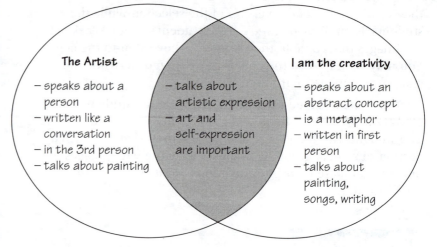

The Artist
- speaks about a person
- written like a conversation
- in the 3rd person
- talks about painting

- talks about artistic expression
- art and self-expression are important

I am the creativity
- speaks about an abstract concept
- is a metaphor
- written in first person
- talks about painting, songs, writing

Using the Venn diagram, discuss the comparison to see if there is a common main idea expressed by both poems.

Ask the students to choose two books, stories, video presentations, or poems they are familiar with and think are similar in some ways, and make a Venn diagram to compare the two to see if they can find a common main idea for both selections.

Writing

Appreciate and Write Metaphors

Blackline Master 3

Have students revisit the poem "I am the creativity" and note the descriptive language the author uses. Invite them to take a second look, and this time identify examples of metaphors such as:
- the paintbrush singing
- the sculpture of the song
- the flame breath of words

A **metaphor,** unlike a simile, does not use "like" or "as" to make a comparison. A metaphor compares by direct statement—by speaking of one thing as if it were another.

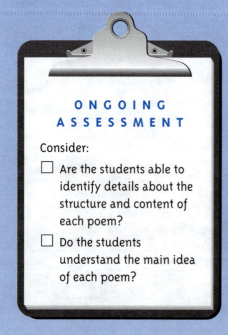

Ask the students to explain why these examples are metaphors—what is being compared directly to what. They could also discuss why authors might use metaphors.

Invite the students to share other examples of metaphors they are familiar with from other selections or ones of their own invention.

– The sea is a waiting lion.
– I am the driver and the wheel.
– Winter has a silvery cloak.
– All the world's a stage.
– She is a peach.

Have the students complete Blackline Master 3, *Meeting Metaphors,* to appreciate, identify, and write examples of metaphors.

 Assessment See **Assess Learning**, page 23.

Blackline Master 3

Visual Communication

 **Paint a Picture**

 mini LESSON

With the students, revisit the selection to look at the illustrations that accompany the poems, as well as other selections in the anthology that have interesting art work/illustrations. Talk about the illustrations, focusing on the illustrator's attention to:

Color
– Do the colors evoke certain feelings or moods?
– Is there a combining of colors to create effect and mood?
– Do the colors go together?

Shapes
– Are shapes bold, straight, strong, curving, soft, or playful?
– Are shapes realistic or abstract representations?
– Do the shapes communicate a message to the viewer?

Have the students paint a picture for one of the poems from this selection, or for another story or poem they have read, or for a piece of their own writing, using any painting technique that they think best matches the selection, such as water-color painting, finger painting, and so on.

Encourage the students to consider the colors and shapes they will use to convey the feelings and mood they want to express in the painting. They may want to talk about their ideas in small groups before beginning their paintings.

Some students might like to draw a painting using a software painting program such as *SuperPaint.* (See pages 5 and (ii) for resource information.)

The finished paintings could be displayed along with the poem or an appropriate excerpt from the story they chose to represent.

LINK TO CURRICULUM

Language Arts

Read Poetry

Some students might like to find and read poems, either by a favorite author or a collection of poems by many authors. Encourage them to choose one or two poems they read that they like and share them with a partner or small group. After sharing the poems, they can talk about what in the poem appeals to them: the language, the subject, the message, ...

Investigate an Artist

Invite the students to create a list of names of local artists or artists from other parts of the country. With a partner or individually, have them choose an artist and gather information about her or him through reference books, the Internet, art galleries, and so on. Suggest that they make jot notes of facts about the artists, such as their interests and accomplishments, where they live/lived, style of their art, what inspires their art, more favored pieces of their art, ...

Some Canadian artists the students could research include Alex Colville, Maude Lewis, Mary Pratt, Ted Harrison, and Emily Carr.

The homework project for Week 1 is to write a report describing a work of art. See *Home Connections Newsletter*, Blackline Master 2.

To share the gathered information, the students could give a talk using their jot notes, showing pictures of the artist's work, if possible.

 If the artist is still living, some students might also like to use the information they gathered to compose and send a FAX message, e-mail, or letter to the artist explaining why they like and appreciate his or her artistic talents.

The Arts

Present Forms of Self-Expression

Ask the students to reread their writing about self-expression (Link to Curriculum), or to think about how they best like to express themselves artistically: writing, painting, drawing, singing, playing music, acting, ..., . They could then choose a form of self-expression and write/draw/paint/... something or develop a short presentation of dance/song/music/readings/...

Encourage the students to work together to plan a way to present their various forms of self-expression to their classmates.

Illustrate Metaphors

Have students revisit their metaphors on their blackline master and choose one or two to illustrate. Suggest that they display their illustrations, along with the written metaphors, so their classmates can view and respond to the visual interpretations.

Assess Learning

Writing (see p. 20)

Ask the students to choose at least two of their metaphors from their blackline master for you to assess. Look for evidence that the student has:

- shown an understanding of metaphors by comparing two unlike things
- demonstrated unique and innovative ways of comparing two things

Use this opportunity to **conference individually** with a few students who, after looking at their samples, you think might benefit from some coaching in using metaphors to compare.

Anger is an erupting volcano.

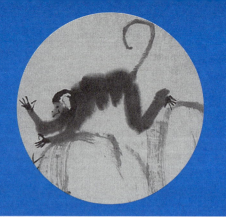

A Young Painter: The Life and Paintings of Wang Yani

This biographical article by Zheng Zhensun and Alice Low is about the extraordinary young Chinese artist, Wang Yani.

Anthology, pages 10-15 **Blackline Masters 4 and 23** **Learning Strategy Card**

Learning Choices

LINK TO EXPERIENCE

Talk About a Mentor

List Ways of Learning How

READ AND RESPOND TO TEXT

READING FOCUS

* summarize and explain the main ideas in information materials, and cite details that support the main ideas
* STRATEGY: **follow along**

REVISIT THE TEXT

READING
Categorize Details
* make judgements and draw conclusions about ideas in written materials on the basis of evidence

WRITING
Write a "Parts of Speech" Poem

* produce pieces of writing using a variety of forms

Language Workshop — Spelling
* affixes; al pattern

VISUAL COMMUNICATION
Create a Picture from Memory
* create a variety of media works

LINK TO CURRICULUM

LANGUAGE ARTS
Make a Poster

THE ARTS
Draw a Picture from a Line

Use Music to Inspire a Painting

SOCIAL STUDIES
Find Out About a Place in China

Key Learning Expectations

Students will
* summarize and explain the main ideas in information materials, and cite details that support the main ideas (**Reading Focus, p. 25**)
* make judgements and draw conclusions about ideas in written materials on the basis of evidence (**Reading Mini Lesson, p. 26**)
* produce pieces of writing using a variety of forms (**Writing Mini Lesson, p. 27**)
* create a variety of media works (**Visual Communication Mini Lesson, p. 29**)

LINK TO EXPERIENCE

Talk About a Mentor

On an index card or piece of paper, ask each student to jot down their ideas in response to these questions:
* Who in your life has taught you how to do something?
* What did they teach or help you to learn?
* How was their help important to you?
* How did you feel towards this mentor?

Have the students form conversation circles to share their responses to the questions.

A **mentor** is an experienced person who guides and teaches another. The relationship is one built on trust.

List Ways of Learning How

Ask the students to think about times when they learned something new and to talk about the strategies/methods they used to learn new things. List their responses.

How We Learn Things

- take lessons
- keep trying over and over again until we get it right
- watch someone do it and imitate him/her
- look at models/pictures
- find information in books

Encourage the students to talk about which ways they learn best, whether they use a combination of ways, if different things need different ways of learning, and so on.

EAD AND RESPOND TO TEXT

Reading Focus

Blackline Master 4

Using the **follow along** strategy, read the first part of the article aloud to the students, stopping at the end of the sentence, "Her favorite music is Chinese music, Beethoven's Fifth Symphony, and works by Schubert and Mozart." Discuss what they have learned about Yani and her father. Work with them to complete the first task on the *Follow Along Grid*, Blackline Master 4.

In pairs, have the students read the rest of the selection, discuss what they learned with their partners, and jot their responses to the prompts on the grid. Then, independently, they can complete the blackline master by using what they have learned to make a web of words/phrases describing Yani and her father.

The students could share and compare their responses and webs in a larger group.

Follow Along Grid(1)

Use this grid to guide you as you read the biography of Wang Yani. At each stopping point, write your responses in your journal.

Read	Write
Read to "Her favorite music is Chinese music, Beethoven's Fifth Symphony, and works by Schubert and Mozart." (p. 11)	1. Describe some of the things Yani does to help her paint. 2. What techniques/methods does Yani use to paint? 3. How did Yani change artistically as she got older?
Read to "He added that he hopes to go back to his own painting when Yani turns eighteen." (p. 12)	4. What did you learn about Yani's father? 5. What else did you learn about Yani and how she paints?
Read to "He adds that it is important to keep that guidance within the boundaries of the child's stage of development." (p. 14)	6. Yani's father guided her growth as an artist in a variety of ways. Describe some of the things he has done.
Read to the end of the biography.	7. What does this last section tell you about Yani? About her father?

Make webs of words and phrases to describe Yani and her father.

Yani   her father

Blackline Master 4

Get Ready to Read

Read the title of the selection and talk about how they will be reading about the life and paintings of a very talented Chinese artist. Ask students to write two or three questions about the artist that they predict will be answered or would like to be answered in the article. Consolidate and list their questions on the board.

Students could
- hold a conversation about the biography to discuss questions such as:
  - **What did you learn about Yani that surprised you? What did you learn about her father that surprised you?**
  - **Do you agree with all the things her father did to help her? Why or why not?**
  - **Would you like to live a life like Yani's? What things would you like? Dislike? Why?**
  - **Have you ever had a mentor? If so, how is Yani's father like a mentor who has helped you? How is he different?**
  - **What did you learn about creativity from this selection?**
- write or draw about a personal experience that is brought to mind by something in the story.
- revisit the list of questions from "Get Ready to Read" to see which ones were answered, and with a partner or small group, answer these questions.
- look at the examples of Yani's paintings, choose their favorite, and try to imitate it using the same style as Yani.
- locate and share information about another child prodigy.

 See **Assess Learning**, page 31.

 **REVISIT THE TEXT**

Reading

Categorize Details

Talk with the students about the organization of the information in the selection, guiding them to note that details about Yani and her life are dispersed throughout the text. To help them organize these details, have them prepare a four-fold organizer by folding a piece of paper into four parts and labelling the parts with these headings:

Yani's painting experiences	Yani's relationship with her father
–	–
–	–
Yani's painting style	Yani's personality/characteristics
–	–
–	–

Ask the students to revisit the selection to find important details about one of the main ideas. Encourage them to scan the entire article for details. Jot the details they find on the board in summary form (rather than sentences from the selection) and note the page numbers where the sentences were found, where appropriate. For example:

> ### Yani's personality/characteristics
> – devoted to her father (throughout the selection)
> – follows her father's advice (throughout the selection)
> – good memory (page 11)
> – thinks for herself, independent (pages 13, 14)
> – humble (page 15)

Review the details the students found, stressing the importance of accessing the entire selection to locate details.

Have the students work in pairs to complete the remaining three sections of their organizers. They can then share their information sheets with other pairs and compare their findings.

Writing

Write a "Parts of Speech" Poem

Learning Strategy Card 40

Write the following poem on the board.

> A dog,
> playful and noisy
> jumps and barks
> excitedly.
> Friend.

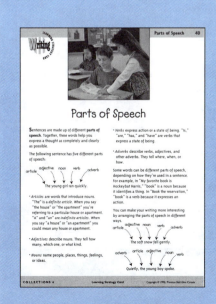

Read the poem to the students and talk about its pattern, eliciting that:

Line 1 – one article and one noun; the name of the subject of the poem

Line 2 – two adjectives describing the subject

Line 3 – two verbs telling what the subject does

Line 4 – one adverb describing how the subject does something

Line 5 – one noun relating to the noun in the first line

While discussing the pattern of the poem, you may wish to use Learning Strategy Card 40, *Parts of Speech*, to review the parts of speech used in the poem.

Ask the students to revisit the selection and choose one of Yani's paintings to use as inspiration for a "Parts of Speech" poem that would describe and tell about the painting from their point of view. As a class, write one or two examples of such poems.

The cranes,
tall and lanky
wading and moving
gracefully.
Birds.

The cranes.
Striking and loud
feeding and nesting
protectively.
Family.

Then ask the students to choose anything they wish and write their own patterned poem about it. The completed poems could be displayed or illustrated and bound in a booklet for the classroom library.

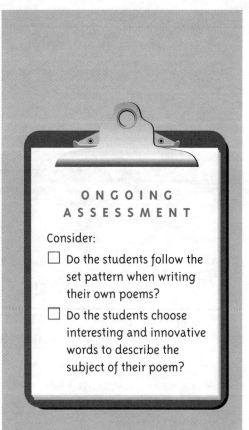

ONGOING ASSESSMENT

Consider:

☐ Do the students follow the set pattern when writing their own poems?

☐ Do the students choose interesting and innovative words to describe the subject of their poem?

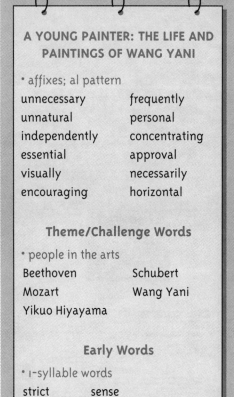

A YOUNG PAINTER: THE LIFE AND PAINTINGS OF WANG YANI

• affixes; al pattern

unnecessary	frequently
unnatural	personal
independently	concentrating
essential	approval
visually	necessarily
encouraging	horizontal

Theme/Challenge Words

• people in the arts

Beethoven	Schubert
Mozart	Wang Yani
Yikuo Hiyayama	

Early Words

• 1-syllable words

strict	sense	
fruit	praise	solve

Blackline Master 23

Explore and Discover

Use Blackline Master 23 and the **sort, share, discuss,** and **chart** procedure outlined on page 17 to work with the words.

In discussing the words, have students note the different suffixes and prefixes. Talk about the meaning of "un" and " in" as used here and in other words they know. Together, consider the words with the pattern "al," discussing which words have a smaller root word and which have "al" as part of the whole word. Words from this spelling list can be used to start or add to spelling pattern charts.

The prefixes "un" and "in" can both be used to mean "not."

Follow this exploration with a **pretest, study and practise,** and a **post test** as outlined on page 17.

Study and Practise

Students could

- use Learning Strategy Card 4 to study words identified after the pretest.
- on the front of the word cards, underline any root words, write them on the back of the card, and check for accuracy.
- put their word cards face down in front of them to play an alphabetical order game in partners or small groups. Working on their own, each student turns over three cards and puts them in alphabetical order. The game continues with each student turning over another card, one at a time, and slotting it into the alphabetical ordering. As soon as a student is finished, he or she copies the ordered words onto a sheet of paper. Another student then checks the list for correct alphabetical order and spelling.

Visual Communication

Create a Picture from Memory

Recall with the students how Yani paints her pictures completely from memory. To help them understand how this can be done, ask them to think of their favorite food. Encourage them to recall in their minds details about the smells, colors, and tastes of the food, the feeling they had when they ate the food, where they ate the food, who was with them, and so on.

Give the students a few quiet minutes to relive their memories, and then ask them to draw their memory. Before they begin to draw, remind them that it is not important to represent all the details of their memory, but to represent their overall impression. They can then share their pictures with a classmate and talk about how visualizing helped them create their pictures.

To extend the activity, take the students on a short excursion around the neighborhood, perhaps visiting a ravine area, a park, ... Ask them to pay attention to the smells, the colors, the sounds, ..., and to their feelings about their surroundings. Upon their return, invite them to take a few minutes to visualize the outing in their minds. Then have them choose one aspect to paint or draw from memory.

LINK TO CURRICULUM

Language Arts

Make a Poster

Ask the students to imagine that Yani will be visiting their community to exhibit her paintings, and they have been asked to design the poster that will be displayed to advertise this special event. Talk about things they will need to think of before they begin their work.
• Where and when will the exhibit take place?
• What information will they include about Yani?
• Will they include a picture of Yani?
• Which of her paintings could be part of the poster?
• What colors could be used to make people take notice and read the poster?
• How should the written information and the art work be organized on the poster?

The students may also wish to look at other posters for upcoming arts events for ideas.

The Arts

Draw a Picture from a Line

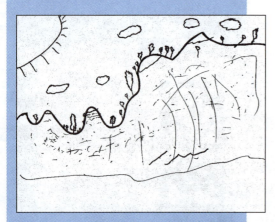

Give each student a large piece of paper and have them draw one bold black line on it. The line could be long and thin, short and curvy, spiral, thick and long,... .Then ask them to look closely at the line, imagine what it could become or be part of, then draw what they "see" using the line as a starting point. Or, the students could draw a line and switch papers with a partner.

Encourage the students to share their art and discuss what made them decide to draw what they did.

Use Music to Inspire a Painting

Recall with the students how Yani listens to music as she paints to stimulate her feelings. Play a piece of music for the students, such as one by Beethoven, Mozart, or Schubert, and have the students paint a picture inspired by the piece. Encourage them to take time to look at their paper and see their painting even before they begin to work, and to think about colors that represent how they feel, the emotion they want to convey, and the impression that they would like to represent.

The students could share the paintings in small groups and discuss how the music stimulated their feelings and their art.

Social Studies

Find Out About a Place in China

Interested students could choose one of the places in China mentioned in the article, or one of their own choosing, to research. Encourage them to use all resources available to them, including print material, the Internet, and people/associations. They could organize the important and interesting information they find into a one-page fact sheet using whatever format they want: question-and-answer format, point form, ..., . They might also want to include illustrations.

The sheets could be displayed or bound into a booklet for the classroom library.

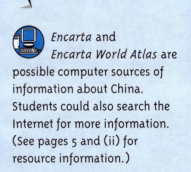

Encarta and *Encarta World Atlas* are possible computer sources of information about China. Students could also search the Internet for more information. (See pages 5 and (ii) for resource information.)

Assess Learning

Assessment

Reader Response (see p. 26)

Plan time to assess the response activities that the students chose. To prepare for the assessment, students could complete a **self-assessment** using the *Reader Response Activity Sheet* from the *COLLECTIONS 6 Assessment Handbook*.

OR

You might prefer to ask all students to write answers to the questions in "hold a conversation" about the selection. Use the written answers as a **work sample** assignment or test of how well the students understood and could relate to the selection.

Note: With some students, you may prefer to hold individual conferences so they can respond orally to the questions.

Carving a Totem Pole

This procedural text by Vickie Jensen provides a great deal of information about how a totem pole is carved and what happens in a pole raising ceremony.

Anthology, pages 16–21
Learning Strategy Card 41

Blackline Masters 5 and 6

Key Learning Expectations

Students will
• summarize and explain the main ideas in information materials, and cite details that support the main ideas **(Reading Focus, p. 33)**
• explain their interpretation of a written work, supporting it with evidence from the work and from their own knowledge and experience **(Reading Mini Lesson, p. 34)**
• use correctly the conventions of punctuation (apostrophe) **(Writing Mini Lesson, p. 35)**
• create a variety of media works (totem pole) **(Visual Communication Mini Lesson, p. 36)**

LINK TO EXPERIENCE

Brainstorm Facts About Totem Poles

Ask the students to think about what they know about totem poles: how they are made, who makes them and why, what the various images on the poles mean, how they are raised, and so on. Organize their ideas on the board or chart paper using a K-W-L chart, listing what the students know under the K (facts we already **k**now) column.

Then ask the students to brainstorm questions they would like answered about totems and list these under the W (what we **w**ant to find out). The L column (what we have **l**earned) could be completed following the reading of the selection.

Talk About a Group Project

Have the students recall a time when they worked with their families, a school group, or any other group to complete a project. They could talk about these projects in groups of three, using questions like the following to help guide their discussion.
• What was the group project?
• Why were you involved with this project?
• What role did you play in helping the group?
• Did the group face any challenges? How were they solved?
• What was the best thing about working together?

Bring the groups together and ask a volunteer from each group to share a few highlights of their discussion.

READ AND RESPOND TO TEXT

Reading Focus

Use a **read and paraphrase** strategy. The students can read the article independently, or listen to the COLLECTIONS audio version, then paraphrase information about the three main parts of the article by jotting key points for each.

Get Ready to Read

Ask the students to read the title of the article and look at the illustrations. Discuss some of the challenges that might be faced in carving and raising a totem pole.

Significance/Kinds of Totem Poles	Carving a Totem Pole	Raising a Totem Pole
– used to teach the history of a people/family	– first designed and drawn on paper	– drum signals are used to help carriers load totem on a long truck
–	–	–

Have the students come together in small groups to share the information they jotted for each of the parts and to discuss and compare the kinds of facts they retrieved from the text.

Reader Response

Students could
- jot ideas in their journals about what their own personal totem pole could tell about.
- complete the L column from the K-W-L chart.
- write or talk about what they found interesting in this story.
- tell a partner about totem poles they have seen.
- read some legends of the Nisga'a people or other First Nations from the west coast.

LEGENDS OF WEST COAST FIRST NATIONS PEOPLES

The Day Sun Was Stolen. Jamie Oliviero. Hyperion Press, 1995.

From First Moon to End of Year. Rosalia Scott. Guinness, 1977.

How Raven Brought Light to People. Ann Dixon. Maxwell Macmillan, 1992.

Orca's Song. Anne Cameron. Harbour, 1987.

Raven Returns to Water. Anne Cameron. Harbour, 1987.

Storm Boy. Paul Owen Lewis. Beyond Words, 1995.

ONGOING ASSESSMENT

Consider:
- ☐ Do the students reread to retrieve key information from the text?
- ☐ Do the students paraphrase the information rather than copying from the text?

Reading

Distinguish Between Main and Supporting Details

Blackline Master 5

The paragraph below provides additional information about the totem pole and its carvers. Copy it onto the board or an overhead. Ask the students to read the paragraph to locate the main or most important detail(s) of the paragraph and the details that support these main detail(s). Suggest that they think about main details as those that contain the ideas/information they would include in a summary of the paragraph.

Once a suitable cedar is found and cut down, the back is sliced off. This massive log will become a doorway totem pole for the Native Education Centre in Vancouver, British Columbia. *Nisga'a artist Norman Tait has been hired to design and carve the pole.* Like carvers in the old days, he relies on the members of his family for his crew. *Norman's youngest brother, Robert "Chip" Tait, will be the foreman.* He is the boss of the other carvers. *Another crew member is Harry" Hammy" Martin, a cousin.* He has done some carving, but this will be his first large pole. *Norman's son, Isaac Tait, and his nephew, Wayne Young, are apprentices who are just learning how to carve.* The crew has three months to carve the 13-metre (42-foot) pole.

Blackline Master 5

With the students, discuss the two kinds of details found in the paragraph (shown here in italics and non-italics) and underline all main details in one color and all supporting details in another color. Discuss with them why both kinds of details are important in text.

Total agreement on what is a main detail and what is a supporting detail is not necessary, but students should be able to provide acceptable reasons for their choices.

For further practice, the students can complete Blackline Master 5, *Main and Supporting Details,* in pairs or independently, and then compare their responses in small groups.

 See **Assess Learning**, page 38.

Writing

Language Workshop — Punctuation

Blackline Master 6
Learning Strategy Card 41

Ask the students to locate examples of words with apostrophes from the article "Carving a Totem Pole" and jot their examples on the board. Talk about the examples, noting that the apostrophe is used in contractions (they'd, couldn't, we're) and to show possession/ownership (Norman's design, Raven's wings, Whale's fin, carver's name,...).

Focusing on the possessives, ask the students to generalize about how each is formed (by adding apostrophe s to the word). Then together, read Learning Strategy Card 41 to find out other ways possessives are formed using an apostrophe. Develop a reference chart, with examples, to consolidate what the students learn.

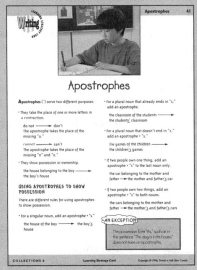

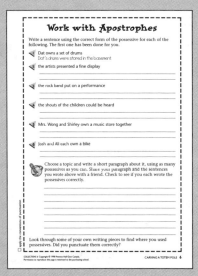

Blackline Master 6

The Apostrophe and Possession

1. Singular and plural nouns that do not end in s, add s (the carver's name, the children's games)
2. Singular nouns that end in s, add apostrophe s (the boss's memo)
3. Names not ending in s, add apostrophe s (Karen's car)
4. Names ending in s, add apostrophe s (James's bike)
5. If two people (groups) possess one thing together, then add apostrophe s or an apostrophe only to the last name (the girls and boys' playground, Ali and Kareem's house)
6. If two people (groups) possess separate things, add apostrophe s to each name (men's and women's bicycles, Bill's and Janis's houses)
7. Do not use an apostrophe with hers, his, its, ours, theirs, and yours because they are already possessive

To refine and extend their understanding, the students can complete Blackline Master 6, *Work with Apostrophes*.

Visual Communication

Create a Model of a Totem Pole

Invite the students to make their own totem pole, but instead of carving it from wood, suggest they design and create it using a variety of materials. For example, the cardboard roll from paper towels could become the "log" for the totem pole, and items such as Plasticine, cloth, empty spools, pipe cleaners, paint, tissue paper, and construction paper could be used to bring life to the totem pole in whatever ways the students decide.

With the students, review the purpose of a totem pole and establish the criteria they could follow as they build their own totem pole. Share and discuss ideas like the following:

- a totem pole can tell a story about a family, an ancestor
- animals are used as symbols in totems; can stand for qualities, characteristics, people
- the order of animals on the pole is important, just like the order of things in a written story
- artists sometimes add a signature piece to say that it is theirs
- the artist draws an outline/design for the totem pole first

Students may want to consult with their own family for ideas of stories that they could build into a totem, and then draw their designs. Have them share and discuss their ideas with a classmate before beginning the model.

Invite the students to meet in small groups to present their totem pole and share its story. Then display all the art pieces, perhaps in the school library.

The students could use a checklist like the following to make sure they have thought of everything before they begin to "carve" their poles.

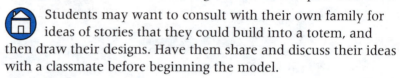

Totem Pole Checklist
_____ I have decided on a story.
_____ I have chosen the animals to symbolize the theme of my story.
_____ I know what order the animals will be placed.
_____ I have decided on what I will use for my signature piece.
_____ I have drawn a plan for the totem pole.
_____ I have shared ideas with a classmate.
_____ I have made any changes I want after talking to my classmate.

Before the students begin their own totem poles, you might like to share some other readings about totem poles with them to reinforce the importance/significance of these in many First Nations' cultures and to provide more information about their design.

BOOKS ABOUT TOTEM POLES

Carving a Totem Pole. Vickie Jensen. Douglas & McIntyre, 1994.

Totem Poles. Diane Hoyt-Goldsmith. Holiday House, 1990.

Whale in the Sky. Anne Siberell. Dutton, 1982.

LINK TO CURRICULUM

Language Arts

Write a News Report

Students could revisit the selection and use information in it to write a news article about the raising of the totem pole that might have appeared in a local newspaper. Encourage them to think about the who, what, when, where, why, and how of news reporting while writing the article. Suggest that they also use quotes to give the article an authentic feeling.

Tell a Story from Pictures

Recall with the students how the totem pole in the selection told a story. Then encourage them to find an interesting picture and make up a story to accompany it. They could choose pictures from magazines, newspapers, or books.

This dog appeared the night I had my birthday party.

After practising, the students could share their stories and pictures with a group of classmates or students in younger grades. Or, they could tape their tellings and place them in the Listening Centre along with the pictures.

Social Studies

Find Out More About Totem Poles

In small groups, the students can brainstorm a list of questions they would like answered about totem poles. Suggest that they refer to their K-W-L chart from "Link to Experience" (if completed) for unanswered questions as a starting point. Once the questions have been generated, suggest that they think of how they will divide up the research, the kinds of resources they can use, what format they will use for their final reporting, and how they will compile all the information into that format.

Questions about Totem Poles

1. What groups/cultures make totem poles? Do people outside of North America make/have made totem poles?
2. Do totems all tell personal stories? Do they have other purposes?
3. Are all of them made of wood? If not, what other materials are used? Are they painted? What kind of paint is used?
4. Are animals the most common symbol used? What others are used? Does each animal always symbolize the same thing?
5. Are all totems big? Where is the world's tallest totem?

Students could search the Internet as well as software programs such as *Totem Poles* to find out more about totem poles. (See pages 5 and (ii) for resource information.)

The Arts

Arrange for a Speaker

A group of interested students could work together to arrange for a speaker to come to the class and talk about native art. The talk could be about art in general or about a specific type of art—carving, sculpture, painting, beadwork, and so on. Suggest that they try contacting a local native organization such as an education centre, or a museum, or an art gallery.

Encourage the students to make a list of tasks that need to be done in arranging for the speaker, during the visit, and following the visit, and to assign various tasks to different group members.

Assess Learning

Reading (see p. 34)

Use the blackline master to hold **individual conferences** with students to assess their ability to correctly identify main and supporting details in text. As you look at and discuss the blackline master together, assess whether students
– identified both main and supporting details
– can provide a rationale for their decisions
– can suggest/make changes if, through this discussion or the one with a partner, they feel some of their decisions may need to be changed

Wildland Visions

In this set of photographs and commentaries about the diversity of Newfoundland and Labrador, Dennis Minty shares his love and respect of the land he calls home.

Anthology, pages 22-26
Learning Strategy Card 42

Blackline Masters 7 and 24

Learning Choices

LINK TO EXPERIENCE

Gather Books About Wildlands

Web Definitions of "Wildland" Words

READ AND RESPOND TO TEXT

READING FOCUS
- explain their interpretation of a written work, supporting it with evidence from the work and from their own knowledge and experience
- STRATEGY: **read, pause, and reflect**

REVISIT THE TEXT

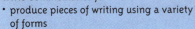

READING
Understand Features of a Personal Photo Essay **Assessment**
- identify a writer's perspective or character's motivation

WRITING **Assessment**
Write Commentaries for Photos
- produce pieces of writing using a variety of forms
Language Workshop — Spelling
- 2- and 3-syllable words; able pattern

VISUAL COMMUNICATION
Develop Skills for Taking Photographs
- create a variety of media works

LINK TO CURRICULUM

LANGUAGE ARTS
Write a Poem

THE ARTS
Design a Logo

SOCIAL STUDIES
Make a Directory

Find Newspaper Clippings

Make a Labelled Map

Key Learning Expectations

Students will
- explain their interpretation of a written work, supporting it with evidence from the work and from their own knowledge and experience **(Reading Focus, p. 40)**
- identify a writer's perspective or character's motivation **(Reading Mini Lesson, p. 41)**
- produce pieces of writing using a variety of forms **(Writing Mini Lesson, p. 42)**
- create a variety of media works **(Visual Communication Mini Lesson, p. 44)**

LINK TO EXPERIENCE

Gather Books About Wildlands

With the students' help, gather a collection of books about the beauty and the purpose of wildlands. Have pairs of students explore the collection and jot a few notes about each resource, perhaps noting how the information is organized, the number of pictures, and so on.

As a whole group, talk about the information they found in the resources and which ones they think they would find the most useful to learn about wildlands.

Web Definitions of "Wildland" Words

List "wildland" words from the selection, along with others, on the board. Have pairs of students choose two and make a definition web for each word. Encourage them to refer to a dictionary and other resources to help them fully understand and define their terms.

bog	bay
island	ecological/ecology
cove	inlet
wetlands	marsh
estuary	natural prairie

Students can share their webs in small groups.

Get Ready to Read

With the students, discuss and list what they know or think they know about the wildlands of Newfoundland and Labrador. Keep the list on the board for reference following the reading of the selection.

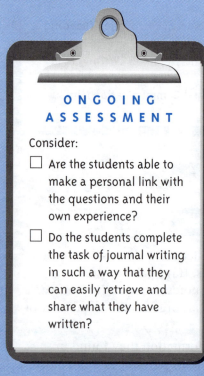

ONGOING ASSESSMENT

Consider:

☐ Are the students able to make a personal link with the questions and their own experience?

☐ Do the students complete the task of journal writing in such a way that they can easily retrieve and share what they have written?

Reading Focus

Use the **read, pause, and reflect** strategy. Independently or in groups of three, students can read the selection in sections, pausing and reflecting on a specific question after each part.

Students working in groups could discuss each question with their classmates first, then write their responses in their journals. Students working independently could write their responses in their journals, then share them with classmates at the end of the selection.

Consider using the following pause points and questions.

Read the first section entitled " Peace of Mind."
Question: If you were to photograph what you loved about your home, your community, or your city, what would two of your photos tell about?

Read the second section entitled "On the Water."
Questions: Can you recall a special time you spent close to water and how it made you feel? Was it with your family? Friends? What things did you do?

Read the third section entitled "Bogs."
Questions: Have you ever visited a bog or another wildland place with many different plants? What did you see? How did you feel?

Read the fourth section entitled " Islands."
Questions: What do you think would be great about living on an island? What do you think might be difficult about living on an island?

Read the last section entitled "Bay du Nord."
Questions: What is your opinion of wilderness areas being taken over by towns and cities? Is there a way to protect the wildness and at the same time establish developments? Explain.

Reader Response

Students could
- revisit the list of information about Newfoundland and Labrador from "Get Ready to Read" and add new information they learned or change any erroneous information.
- choose the photo they liked the best and write about it in their journals, telling what is special about it.
- tell about a personal experience they are reminded of by one of the photos or messages written by the photographer.

- jot questions they could ask the photographer in order to learn about his approach to taking photos.
- make a list of photos they would take to share their feelings about a topic close to them, such as special people, fun times, their homes, ..., .
- search the *Canadian Encyclopedia* or *Adventure Canada* for more information about Newfoundland and Labrador and/or search the Internet for Newfoundland's provincial home page. (See pages 5 and (ii) for resource information.)

REVISIT THE TEXT

Reading

Understand Features of a Personal Photo Essay

Explain to the students that this selection is an example of a unique way of sharing images, information, and feelings about a topic through photographs/images and minimal text. Discuss questions such as:
- What topic did the author choose for his photos/commentaries? Does he have strong feelings about the topic? How do you know?
- What do you think was the author's purpose in creating this selection? Did he want to present a strong message, shake up, and/or inspire the viewer?
- Is there an order to the photographs or could they be viewed in any order?
- Does the text strengthen the impact of the photos?

Summarize the discussion by establishing key factors of this selection:
- the topic is personal and important to the author
- the author has a purpose in creating the selection
- the photos can be viewed in any order, but together form a diverse collection of photos about the topic
- the text adds a personal dimension to the photos

 Invite the students to begin preparing their own set of photos for a personal photo essay similar to Dennis Minty's by first choosing a topic that they care about. Some students may be able to take new photos for their essay, while others may prefer to ask family members for help in looking through existing snapshots for appropriate photos. As well, some students may need to use magazines to find appropriate pictures for their essay.

Once the students have gathered a number of photos/pictures, suggest they choose five or six that best show what they want to impart to the viewer about their topics.

 See **Assess Learning**, page 46.

 The homework project for Week 2 is to interview people for opinions about how natural areas can be preserved in their community. See *Home Connections Newsletter*, Blackline Master 2.

The viewing/representing mini lesson for this selection focuses on the criteria of good photographs. You may prefer to complete that lesson before the students begin shooting/choosing photos/pictures.

As well, in the following writing mini lesson, the students will write the commentaries for their photos. The completed project from this lesson and the writing lesson is the focus of the "Assess Learning" suggestion.

Writing

Write Commentaries for Photos

Read aloud one of the section's accompanying text as the students follow in their books. Discuss the ways the author wrote the text so as to enhance and extend the images in the photos. List their ideas about his writing style. Some responses might be:
– written in the first person
– personal feelings expressed
– related to past experiences
– mixed personal stories with facts about the topic
– used descriptive language to build on images
– tone was warm and conversational

Take time to discuss each element of the author's style and how it worked together with the photos to convey a message to the readers/viewers.

Encourage the students to use Dennis Minty's informal approach for writing photo text to write commentaries for their photos. Suggest that they refer to the list of ideas and/or reread the selection's text before they begin composing.

The commentaries and photos could be arranged on a piece of poster board and displayed in the classroom. Remind the students to think about the "total look" they want to achieve with their photo essay before attaching pieces to the poster board.

Assessment   See **Assess Learning**, page 46.

Students could create their personal photo essays using a program such as the video workshop on *Multimedia Workshop,* where they can create scenes by laying out photographs, then combining the scenes and sounds together on the storyboard grid. (See pages 5 and (ii) for resource information.)

Blackline Master 24

Explore and Discover

Use Blackline Master 24 and the **sort, share, discuss,** and **chart** procedure outlined on page 17 to work with the words.

In discussing the words, have the students clap out the number of syllables in each word and indicate when a word has a pattern they are familiar with in one of the syllables.

Write the words from the list with the "able" pattern, along with others students can recall. Use some of these words in sentences and talk about how they are used as descriptive words. Point out how in "recognizable," the silent "e" is dropped. Ask the students if this is true of any of the additional words they suggested. An ongoing chart can be started or added to for the "able" pattern.

> The suffix "able" generally makes the word an adjective that describes an attribute or effect.

Follow this exploration with a **pretest, study and practise,** and a **post test** as outlined on page 17.

Study and Practise

Students could
- use Learning Strategy Card 4 to study words identified after the pretest.
- use a print or electronic dictionary to confirm where the syllabic divisions are in the words to study, and write the words, in syllables, on the back of the word cards
- choose ten words and list them in random order, numbering them from zero to nine. They then write their phone number vertically, and beside each letter, write the word in their list that has been given the corresponding number.

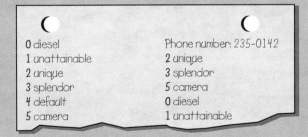

0 diesel
1 unattainable
2 unique
3 splendor
4 default
5 camera

Phone number: 235-0142
2 unique
3 splendor
5 camera
0 diesel
1 unattainable

WILDLAND VISIONS

• 2- and 3-syllable words; able pattern

unattainable	reserve	tribute
camera	reasonable	supreme
tropical	unique	diesel
default	splendor	(splendour)
recognizable		

Theme/Challenge Words

• wildland words

Bay du Nord	sponges
bounteous	bladderworts
ecological	

Early Words

• double letters

struggle	freedom
choose	occur
between	

You may wish to use school cameras, or have students bring their own, for this activity. A number of pairs could use the same camera and roll of film.

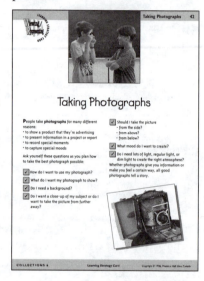

Blackline Master 7

Consider inviting a local photographer to the class to talk about the techniques involved in taking a good photograph and to show the students examples of different kinds of photos (portraits, landscapes, ...).

Visual Communication

Develop Skills for Taking Photographs

Blackline Master 7
Learning Strategy Card 42

Arrange the students in small groups and provide each group with a number of photographs and/or pictures of photographs. Ask each group to evaluate and categorize each one as a good photo, a passable photo, or a poor photo.

Bring the groups together to share their photos and reasons for their evaluations; for example, a good photo could be one where the scene was balanced, easily viewed, and not complicated by a busy background. Then discuss Learning Strategy Card 42 with the students to help them learn more about ideas they could use when they take a photograph.

Pairs of students could work together to take a few planned photographs. They could use Blackline Master 7, *Taking a Photograph,* to help them plan their photos. When the photos have been developed, have the partners compare the results of the photo with their plan.

LINK TO CURRICULUM

Language Arts

Write a Poem

Ask the students to choose their favorite picture from the selection or one from their own personal photo essay and compose a poem about it. Suggest that they first web or list action/descriptive words and phrases that the photo evokes. Encourage them to recall the variety of poetic patterns they are familiar with and select one that would best fit their writing style and the topic of the poem.

The Arts

Design a Logo

Students could brainstorm a list of logos they have seen and discuss what message was conveyed by the design of the logos. They could then design a logo for a club that has as its mandate the preservation of wildlands. Encourage them to think about the message they want to send to the public and incorporate a design that would enhance the message.

Display the logos so the students can view them and discuss the designs.

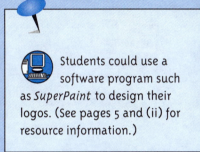

Students could use a software program such as *SuperPaint* to design their logos. (See pages 5 and (ii) for resource information.)

Social Studies

Make a Directory

Interested students could look through a variety of resources, such as the telephone book, web sites, magazines, and pamphlets to find people and organizations that work toward the preservation of wildlands, wildlife, nature, and so on. They could organize the information into a directory with the organizations and resource people listed along with a description/explanation of their work's focus. The directory could be placed in the school library.

Find Newspaper Clippings

Some students could read through their local newspapers looking for articles and information on issues and concerns about the preservation of nature. The clippings could be displayed on a bulletin board that could continue over a period of time as older news is replaced with current clippings.

Make a Labelled Map

Students could work in a group to find out about some interesting places in Newfoundland and Labrador, like Bay du Nord. Suggest that they write the name and a bit of information about each place on a label and attach the labels in the correct location on a large blank map of the province. They could make the large map by using an overhead or opaque projector to project a small map onto a large sheet of paper and trace the outline.

Using a program such as *Encarta World Atlas,* students can add electronic "pushpins" (similar to Post-its or labels) to identify interesting places in Newfoundland. (See pages 5 and (ii) for resource information.)

Assess Learning

Reading/Writing (see p. 41 and p. 42)

Appoint various teams of three to four students to work together to **peer assess** a completed photo essay, ensuring that all students have an opportunity to participate in an assessment. Discuss, collaborate on, and post criteria in advance.

For example, the groups of students could use a rating scale similar to the following, with 1 being the lowest and 5 the highest. The assessment could be stored in each student's portfolio.

Rating Scale for Photo Essay

1. Photos/Commentaries had a clear purpose/message.	1	2	3	4	5
2. Photos were appropriate for the topic/message.	1	2	3	4	5
3. Photos showed a variety of things about the topic.	1	2	3	4	5
4. Commentaries added both personal and factual information about the photos.	1	2	3	4	5
5. Photos/Commentaries were displayed in an interesting and appealing way.	1	2	3	4	5

Comments: _____

A Musical Note — *a personal narrative*

Painting — *an essay*

Music in My Life — *a personal narrative*

LINK TO THE THEME

After the students read the selections aloud in small groups, or listen to the *COLLECTIONS* audio version, invite them to

- make a personal connection with one of the pieces of writing and tell about the experience.
- discuss how the writers invite you into their writing by expressing their personal feelings about the topic.

LINK TO THE WRITING PROCESS

Write a Personal Narrative

Discuss "A Musical Note" and "Music in My Life" to note the common elements between them. Ask students to reread the selections to find where the writers express their strong personal feelings by providing specific examples and descriptive wording.

Students can then think of a topic that evokes strong emotions for them and write personal narratives that include their feelings about the topic and provide personal examples.

Language Workshop — Style

- use writing for various purposes and in a range of contexts, including school work

Blackline Master 8

Teach/Explore/Discover

Write the following sentences on the board or on an overhead transparency. Discuss the difference, guiding the students to realize that one sentence is rich with descriptive language, while the other merely expresses the bare facts.

1. Whether my fingers move across the keys or whether they lace up my boots, music has brought much to my life.

2. Whether my fingers are guided gently across the black and ivory keys of the piano, or whether they're reaching out to carefully lace up my worn leather jazz boots, music has brought such colorful tones to my life.

Invite the students to reread the remainder of the selection, "A Musical Note," and look for how the writer continues to use rich and descriptive language. Point out to the students that when writing a personal topic that includes descriptive language, the author helps the reader see, hear, and sense the true feelings and voice of the writer.

Practise/Apply

Students could

- complete Blackline Master 8, *Write with Description*.
- revisit a piece of their own writing to add vivid and descriptive language.

Blackline Master 8

LINK TO THE WRITER

Ashley Buczkowski's comments describe what she likes best about writing and why in particular she enjoys writing about music— she wants to share her love of music.

Students can review their portfolios and reflect on which piece they most enjoyed writing. Ask them to write a comment explaining why they enjoyed it and their purpose for writing the piece. The comments could be posted along with the students' chosen selections.

Get Set for the Net!

This selection is taken from *CyberSurfer: The Owl Internet Guide for Kids* by Nyla Ahmad. It traces the history of communication from the telegraph to the Internet, concluding with cyberspace terms and information about the working of the I-Way.

Anthology, pages 28-34   Blackline Master 9
Learning Strategy Card 43

Learning Choices

LINK TO EXPERIENCE

Talk About the Word "Net"

Write About a Way of Communicating

READ AND RESPOND TO TEXT

READING FOCUS
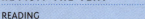
• summarize and explain the main ideas in information materials, and cite details that support the main ideas
• STRATEGY: **follow along**

REVISIT THE TEXT

READING
Connect Summarizing Statements and Details
• read a variety of fiction and non-fiction materials for different purposes

WRITING
Present Information in Various Formats
• produce pieces of writing using a variety of forms, techniques, and resources appropriate to the form and purpose, and materials from other media

VISUAL COMMUNICATION
Make a Flow Chart or Map
• create a variety of media works

LINK TO CURRICULUM

LANGUAGE ARTS
Write a Script

TECHNOLOGY
Conduct Research on the Internet

Find Out About Early Computers

SOCIAL STUDIES
Learn About Earth Day

Research an Inventor

Key Learning Expectations

Students will
• summarize and explain the main ideas in information materials, and cite details that support the main ideas (**Reading Focus, p. 49**)
• read a variety of fiction and non-fiction materials for different purposes (**Reading Mini Lesson, p. 49**)
• produce pieces of writing using a variety of forms, techniques, and resources appropriate to the form and purpose, and materials from other media (**Writing Mini Lesson, p. 50**)
• create a variety of media works (**Visual Communication Mini Lesson, p. 51**)

LINK TO EXPERIENCE

Talk About the Word "Net"

Invite the students to brainstorm a variety of ways in which the word "net" can be applied to the Internet. Encourage them to use their imaginations as well as factual information they know. Jot their ideas on the board in a web or list.

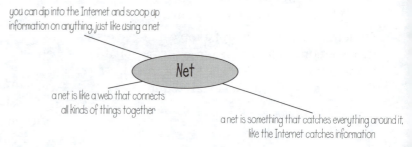

you can dip into the Internet and scoop up information on anything, just like using a net

Net

a net is like a web that connects all kinds of things together

a net is something that catches everything around it, like the Internet catches information

Write About a Way of Communicating

Put the terms telegraph, satellite dish, typewriter, telephone, phonograph, radio, motion pictures, and video conference on the board or overhead. Ask the students to choose one and write a short paragraph telling what they know about that form of communication.

Students could then get together in small groups to share what they wrote and add any new ideas they get from the group members to their paragraphs.

READ AND RESPOND TO TEXT

Reading Focus

Blackline Master 9

Students can use a **follow along** strategy to read the article independently and respond to the questions on Blackline Master 9. After the reading, they can share their responses with a partner.

Blackline Master 9

Reader Response

Students could:
- hold a conversation to discuss questions such as:
  - **How did earlier inventions and advances lead to or connect to today's technology?**
  - **How do you think people felt about the earlier communication inventions? How do you think people view the Internet today?**
  - **How have you used the Internet?**
  - **How is information on the Internet the same as what you find in books, magazines, newspapers? How is it different?**
  - **What new ways of communication do you see for the future?**
- in small groups, complete the K-W-L chart by listing the new things they learned about the Internet from this article.
- gather books with information about the Internet written for younger people and use these books to help answer any further questions they have.
-  research Morse Code (possibly using the Internet!) and use it to send short messages to each other.

REVISIT THE TEXT

mini LESSON

Reading

Connect Summarizing Statements and Details

Have the students look at the techno-history survey on pages 29-31, noting how it is set up with an accomplishment of the 1800s across the top, one from the 1900s across the bottom, and detailed information in the middle. ▶

Get Ready to Read

As a group, have the students begin a K-W-L chart, listing what they already know about the Internet and what they'd like to know. After reading the article, they can add what they learned about the Internet in the third column of the chart.

ONGOING ASSESSMENT

Consider:
- ☐ Do the students show an appreciation for inventions of the past and see how they played a part in leading to the present technology?
- ☐ Can the students articulate what they learned about the Internet?

Together, work with the "Electronic Messages" section. Write the dates and statements as headings on the board or overhead, noting that these statements summarize briefly the great advancement in communication made in that year. Have the students read the paragraph for more information and determine which details are connected to each of the summary statements. List these under the statements. Discuss the relationship between the information in the paragraph and the statement, and the importance of both.

1844 Morse invents the telegraph and sends the first electronic message.

– Samuel Morse invented the telegraph in 1844
– words could be sent quickly over long distances over telegraph wires
– key pressed to send electronic pulses that made dots and dashes to spell out the words
–

1946 The Electronic Numerical Integrator and Calculator (ENIAC) begins to operate. ·

– first computer invented 100 years after telegraph
– also transmitted a code of pulses
–

In pairs, the students could choose one of the other segments of the timeline and list the summary statements and details. They could then compare their lists with another pair who chose the same segment.

Writing

Present Information in Various Formats

The viewing/representing mini lesson for this selection focuses on flow charts/maps. You may wish to do this writing lesson following the viewing/representing lesson so that the students have a more complete understanding of this format.

Have the students look through the article and note the various formats in which information is presented—sections of text (from one paragraph to many), survey of historical events, riddles, flow chart/map. List these as students mention them and talk about:
• the effectiveness of each type of format
• the kinds of information that are particularly suited for each format
• how the style of writing might change when using a certain format
• how the variety of the formats makes the selection more interesting to read.

Together, create a wall reference chart showing the different types of formats. Add any other formats the students know of to the chart.

Encourage the students to use a variety of formats the next time they write a report, either in this unit or in another curriculum area such as social studies or science.

Ask the students to look again at the map of the I-Way (p. 33). Invite them to share what they learned from the map as they went through it on their own. Together, go through the flow of it, perhaps having the students follow with their fingers. Talk about the different icons and the explanations provided in the legend, and discuss how the map shows the interconnectedness of the elements on the I-Way.

Have students brainstorm other things that are/could be represented in the same way. They might think of such things as the electrical wiring of a home, a city's sewer system, underground passages connecting different places, a subway system, a map showing places of interest and how to get to them, routes various students use to get from their homes to school, and hallways and rooms of the school. Choose one of their ideas and together, do a quick sketch of a flow chart or map, complete with arrows and a legend.

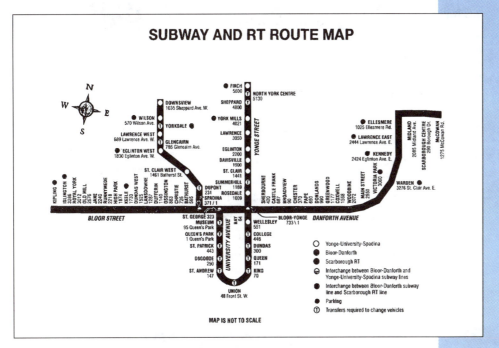

Students can work in small groups to create maps of something of their own choosing that involve interconnected pathways and places. When the maps are completed, have each group share and explain them to the class. They could then be displayed in the hallway for other classes to enjoy.

 See **Assess Learning**, page 53.

LINK TO CURRICULUM

Language Arts

Write a Script

Students could select a quotation from "Famous First Words," imagine what happened before and after the message was sent, and write a script for a scene to portray the conversation and activity that might have happened around those words. They could then work with a partner or small group to perform the scene for others.

Technology

Conduct Research on the Internet

Learning Strategy Card 43

Encourage the students to follow their interests in music, art, or drama and find interesting and appropriate material on the Internet, at home or at school. Or, they may wish to choose another area they are interested in. Prior to the activity, have them read Learning Strategy Card 43 on search engines to help them with their research.

The students could share their findings with others in small groups and recommend websites that provide particularly good reading, viewing, or listening about their chosen area.

Find Out About Early Computers

Interested students could talk to people to find out about early computers, both mainframe and personal. Encourage them to check with a variety of people, such as people at computer stores, communications agencies, friends, family members, and so on. They could then get together as a group and consolidate what they find into a timeline, written report, chart, or other format of their choice, showing the changes in computers over the years.

Social Studies

Learn About Earth Day

Using resources such as the Internet, newspaper, magazines, local agencies, and so on, the students could find out about Earth Day—its history, purpose, and activities. They can then make posters advertising and providing information about the next celebration of Earth Day.

To extend the activity, some students may wish to begin planning their own project for this significant day.

Research an Inventor

Students could select one of the people mentioned in the techno-history survey, or another inventor of interest, and write a report telling about his/her life, the development of a particular invention, other inventions he/she is credited with, and so on. These reports can be put up on the bulletin board or compiled into a reference booklet entitled "Great Inventors."

 To gain a better understanding of inventions and the process that inventors typically follow, students might want to visit the web site "Invention and Design" at:
http://www.bergen.org/ECEMS/class/welcome.html

Assess Learning

Visual Communication (see p. 51)

As each group shows and explains their map or flow chart, use a **checklist** to assess the map/chart under headings such as:
• interconnected pathways
• directional arrows
• places, objects, and/or destinations
• legend and definitions

As well, make **anecdotal comments** about the clarity and sense of connectiveness shown in both the map itself and in the oral explanation. The maps can be handed in as **work samples** of a group project.

Fast Forward Art

This selection features student art and commentaries selected from the entries in the "Under 13" category of the *Toronto Star's* Fast Forward Digital Art Competition.

Anthology, pages 35-39   Blackline Master 24
Learning Strategy Card 44

Learning Choices

LINK TO EXPERIENCE

List Ways of Creating Art Pieces

Talk About Computer Terms

READ AND RESPOND TO TEXT

READING FOCUS
• explain their interpretation of a written work, supporting it with evidence from the work and from their own knowledge and experience **Assessment**
• STRATEGY: **read and conect**

REVISIT THE TEXT

mini LESSONS

READING
Make an Information Matrix
• read independently, selecting appropriate reading strategies

WRITING
Write an Introduction **Assessment**
• select words and expressions to create specific effects
Language Workshop — Spelling
• -ed, -ity, -ly patterns

VISUAL COMMUNICATION
Compare Digital Art Pieces
• analyze and assess a media work and express a considered viewpoint about it

LINK TO CURRICULUM

LANGUAGE ARTS/TECHNOLOGY
Write/Give Instuctions

Critique Computer Programs

THE ARTS
Sponsor a Digital Art Display/Contest

SOCIAL STUDIES
Learn About Digital Art in Movies

Key Learning Expectations

Students will
• explain their interpretation of a written work, supporting it with evidence from the work and from their own knowledge and experience (**Reading Focus, p. 55**)
• read independently, selecting appropriate reading strategies (**Reading Mini Lesson, p. 55**)
• select words and expressions to create specific effects (**Writing Mini Lesson, p. 56**)
• analyze and assess a media work and express a considered viewpoint about it (**Visual Communication Mini Lesson, p. 58**)

LINK TO EXPERIENCE

List Ways of Creating Art Pieces

Ask the students to brainstorm all the ways they can think of to create art pieces: drawings, paintings, sculptures, collages, models, ..., along with different mediums that can be used: oil paints, charcoal, marble, papier-mâché, steel, ..., . Jot their ideas in a web or chart. Then ask each student to choose one medium, such as oil painting, and write or talk about what they like about the medium and something they have created or would like to create in that way.

Talk About Computer Terms

Write some computer terms/programs on the board. Ask the students to share what they know about any of these and other terms/programs they know that relate to doing art on computers.

digital art   MS Paint
                              mouse
                                        cut and paste
        gradients

Fractal Design Dabbler 1.0   clip art   zoom in mode

READ AND RESPOND TO TEXT

Reading Focus

Students can use a **read and connect** strategy to read the artists' commentaries and look closely at their digital art. As they read and view, ask them to select four pieces that they particularly like, can relate to personally in some way, or would like to try to create themselves.

Following the reading, arrange the students in small groups to share their choices and the reasons for their choices.

Reader Response

Students could
- write in their journals about their feelings and experience with digital art: what they like or don't like, the advantages and disadvantages of it, programs they've used, ..., .
- in a small group, talk about movies or cartoons they've seen that used digital art.
- think about how their personal art expression has changed over the years and, if possible, make a scrapbook of art pieces to show the changes.
- choose an art piece they have recently completed and write a commentary about it similar to the ones in the selection.
- with a small group, make a list of criteria they would use to judge digital art and discuss which piece from the selection they would have chosen as the winner using those criteria.

REVISIT THE TEXT

Reading

Make an Information Matrix

Have the students skim through the selection to determine the different types of information provided in the artists' commentaries. Talk with them about how to form a matrix, and together, choose headings for the types of information that could be used for the rows of a matrix. Using these headings and the names of two of the artists for the column headings, begin the outline of a matrix on the board or overhead.

▶

Get Ready to Read

Write the title "Fast Forward Art" on the board and invite students to suggest what they think it means and what the selection might be about.

ONGOING ASSESSMENT

Consider:
- ☐ Can the students make a personal connection to some of the works?
- ☐ Do the students' comments show an understanding of the artists' uses and enjoyment of digital art?

The criteria the students generate could be used in looking at digital art pieces created in the Link to Curriculum activity "Sponsor a Digital Art Display/Contest."

With the students, fill in the matrix for these two artists. Note how each heading at the side of the matrix does not always apply to all the artists, and therefore, some boxes are left blank.

	Kenneth Yan (age 11)	Hinal Pithia (age 6)	
Picture Title	Space	Landscape	
Why subject was chosen		– loves to paint things of nature	
Computer program, tools, or features	– eraser – "Lighting Effect" – "Gradients"	– mouse – many colors	
Reasons for liking digital art	– not so boring – lots of options – saves time	– can use so many colors	
Additional information	– doesn't like drawing normally	– would like a color printer	

Creating a matrix is one way to organize and compare information about a number of things, and students can use this strategy as a way of organizing, comparing, and/or studying in other curricular areas.

Have the students complete the matrix for four other artists on their own or with a partner, and then share them in a small group.

Writing

Write an Introduction

Learning Strategy Card 44

Invite a volunteer to read aloud the introduction to this selection, while others listen to note what information is presented and how it is set out. Talk with the students about the introduction, list the features and structures they note, and organize these in a chart.

Ask the students to read Learning Strategy Card 44 and to look at other introductions in this anthology and various materials currently being used, and add additional points to the chart.

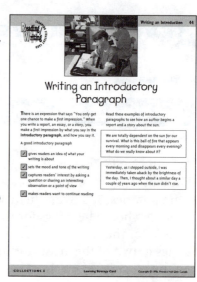

Features and Structure of an Introduction

1. Opening
   - something to catch your attention or draw you into the topic
   - may be a reflective thought, definition, exclamation, question, ...
2. Middle
   - provides some background information about the topic
   - might have a question to think about as you read
   - may briefly outline what's coming
3. Closing
   - leads you into reading the rest of the article or story
   - may be an explanation, question, or a challenge
4. Other Points
   - can be very short or a few paragraphs, but usually not too long
   - sometimes you get the feeling the writer is talking to you

Ask the students to choose a piece of their own writing from any curricular area that they could write an introduction for, such as a report, article, introductory page to a booklet, story, diagram, chart, ..., .

 Assessment See **Assess Learning**, page 60.

You may wish to ask the students to write an introduction for an activity they complete in the Link to Curriculum suggestions for this selection. They could also write an introduction for the matrix they completed in the "Make an Information Matrix" lesson.

Language Workshop — Spelling • -ed, -ity, -ly patterns

Blackline Master 24

Explore and Discover

Use Blackline Master 24 and the **sort, share, discuss**, and **chart** procedure outlined on page 17 to work with the words.

In discussing the words, work with students to write the root words and group them according to changes made before adding the suffix. Choose a few words to build word webs around, and ask students to write sentences using some words from the webs.

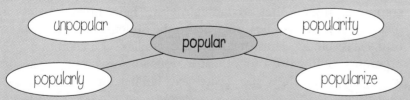

Follow this exploration with a **pretest, study and practise,** and a **post test** as outlined on page 17.

FAST FORWARD ART

• -ed, -ity, -ly patterns

published	demonstrated
normally	wonderfully
popularity	modified
inspired	accurately
originality	especially
quality	reproduced

Theme/Challenge Words

• Internet words (from "Get Set for the Net!")

protocol	modulator
modem	cyberspace
emoticon	

Early Words

• er pattern

modern	interesting
patterns	everyone
computer	

Study and Practise

Students could
- use Learning Strategy Card 4 to study words identified after the pretest.
- sort their cards into two piles: "words I know for sure" and "words I need to study." On the word cards they need to study, they can highlight tricky parts and write the root word on the back of the card.
- create word webs for at least four words they need to study.

Visual Communication

Compare Digital Art Pieces

Select two pieces of digital art from the selection and, with the students, talk about the features of the art such as subject, style, techniques, and elements of design (color, lines, ...). Have the students consider similarities and differences between the two pieces. This comparison can be summarized in a Venn Diagram, comparison chart, or in written paragraphs.

Students can work on their own or in pairs to look at the features of two other digital art pieces, and compare them using one of the above choices of format.

LINK TO CURRICULUM

Language Arts/Technology

Write/Give Instructions

 Students can write and illustrate step-by-step instructions for using a particular digital art program or for any computer program they are familiar with. Their illustrated instruction pages can be displayed on the bulletin board or put into a class binder. Those students not familiar with computer programs could write a set of instructions for some other technology they know about, such as a fax machine, a VCR, a camcorder, ..., .

Or, the students could read a set of instructions and present them orally to a small group, using illustrations or the actual program/machine to show the steps in the instructions.

> If the students do the "Sponsor a Digital Art Display/Contest" in Link to Curriculum, they could follow up with a comparison of two art pieces of their choosing.

Critique Computer Programs

Students who have worked with digital art programs can write a critique of a program, assessing its features, ease of use, and the effects that can be achieved, and offer recommendations for certain purposes or for certain users. Students familiar with programs other than digital art ones, may wish to write a critique of them.

The Arts

Sponsor a Digital Art Display/ Contest

Interested students could work together to plan a digital art display or contest for students in the school or selected grades. Suggest that they set up guidelines for the participants' entries, and make arrangements for displaying, critiquing (if they choose to), and honoring the works.

Students could use a software program such as *Creative Writer 2* to design posters advertising the display/contest, to post around the school. (See pages 5 and (ii) for resource information.)

HONORING OUR DIGITAL ARTISTS

Sun

Social Studies

Learn About Digital Art in Movies

Some students might like to work in small groups to find out about digital art techniques used in movies, or about how they were used in one specific movie, or about one particular digital art artist. Encourage each group to use a variety of sources to get their information and to find illustrations to enhance their report. Each group's findings could be displayed on a large sheet of bristol board, and then compiled into a big book, complete with introduction and table of contents.

Writing (see p. 56)

Collect as **work samples,** introductions students have written for a report, article, or activity connected with "Fast Forward Art" or another curricular area. Before handing in their introduction, have students complete a **self-assessment** checklist to verify their use of some of the organizational features and structures. This checklist can be attached to their work sample.

Introduction Checklist

Name:_____

	Good	Needs Work
Opening – catches the readers' attention or draws them into the topic – includes a reflective thought, definition, exclamation, question, _____, (circle one)		
Middle – provides background – has a question to think about – briefly outlines what's coming		
Closing – leads reader into the rest of the article or story – includes an explanation, question, or challenge (circle one)		
Other Points – not too long; a few sentences or paragraphs – gives the feeling I am talking to the reader		

Teacher Comments:_____

_____

World Shrinkers

For this article, Lynn Bryan interviewed students from classes in two schools involved in communication projects. These students use video conferencing and e-mail to shrink distances between themselves and others.

Anthology, pages 40-44

Key Learning Expectations

Students will
• read a variety of fiction and non-fiction materials for different purposes (**Reading Focus, p. 62**)
• identify a writer's perspective or character's motivation (**Reading Mini Lesson, p. 63**)
• select words and expressions to create specific effects (**Writing Mini Lesson, p. 64**)
• follow up on others' ideas, and recognize the validity of different points of view in group discussions or problem-solving activities (**Oral Communication Mini Lesson, p. 64**)

LINK TO EXPERIENCE

Categorize Ways of Learning About People

Ask the students to brainstorm ways in which they learn about people and/or get to know them better. They may suggest such ways as talking, doing things together, interviewing, writing letters, sending e-mail messages, reading biographies and autobiographies, talking to someone who knows them, observing them, looking at photograph albums, and so on.

Make a list of their suggestions and ask the students to categorize them according to personal/impersonal or other criteria they may choose.

Talk About E-Mail Addresses

Ask the students to share some e-mail addresses they know and write them on the board or overhead. Group together ones that are similar and note any patterns or features that seem to be common in all the addresses. Talk about what the different parts of the address mean or what their function is. Choose one address and label its parts for reference.

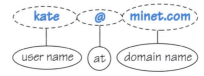

READ AND RESPOND TO TEXT

Get Ready to Read

Read aloud the introduction to the article and ask the students to share what they know about e-mail, the Internet, faxes, and video conferencing. Ask them to note as they read how some of these communication systems are being used by students in schools to "shrink the distances between themselves and others."

Information about Lyle Weis's on-line editing workshops is available by writing him at:
  11607– 49 Ave. Edmonton, AB. T6H 0G9
  e-mail: tales@oanet.com

A Special Gift
The students in Mr. Milson's class went on a camping trip to Jasper, Alberta. Each student had their picture taken at some point on the trip. The class compiled a coil bound book of the pictures, with explanations about each picture, and sent it to their Australian keypals as an end-of-the-year gift.

Reading Focus

Use a variation of the **double look** strategy. Have the students first read the article independently to get a general impression of how the students in both projects are drawing closer together through technology. Then have them read the article a second time to find and jot answers to questions such as the following:
- Describe how the video conferences operate in "Project Interact."
- Which part of the project would you like better—the editing session with the author or with other students? Give reasons for your choice.
- What advantages does communicating by e-mail have over regular mail?
- List six things you learned about Australia from the keypal letters.

The students could share their jot notes in small groups.

Reader Response

Students could
- hold a conversation about the article to discuss questions such as:
  - **What improvements do you think the students would see in their writing after they had been involved with "Project Interact" for a few months?**
  - **What could the students do to help ensure their keypal relationships are successful?**
  - **What things of interest would you tell keypals from Australia about and why?**
  - **Have you ever had a keypal or penpal? Would you like to have one? Why or why not?**
  - **What other new technologies are helping to shrink the world?**
  - **What are some further uses of technology that could help learning and communicating in schools (for example, connecting with the public library through fax or e-mail)?**
- as a group, make a scrapbook about their school and community to send to another school in a community of their choice (see margin note).
- investigate the possibilities of inviting an author, parent, or other volunteer to come to their classroom to help them with editing their writing.
- learn more about the technology used in the two schools in the article.
- with a group, make a list of projects the class could do using whatever technology is available in their school that would shrink the miles between them and another group of students.

Reading

Determine Questions and Answers

Have the students skim through the article and locate questions that the author wrote to help focus the reader on what is going to come next or to summarize/comment on what has just been written. Write these on the board:

> – ... and what do you get?
> – What kind of conference is most useful?
> – What about their peer editors?
> – Where in the world is Port Fairy?
> – Incredible isn't it?
> – What other communication projects lie ahead for the keypals and the students of Project Interact?

With the students, choose one of the questions and have the students read the text around the question to find details connected to the question. Jot these on the board; for example:

Where in the world is Port Fairy?

– halfway around the world from Edmonton
– on the south eastern tip of Australia
– in the state of Victoria
– it takes 17 hours to get there by plane
– a letter takes about 2 weeks
– an e-mail message goes in minutes

Have students reread "Project Interact" on pages 40-42 and, as a group, think of questions that could be used as headings under which important information in the section could be listed. List these on the board and ask the students to find details for each question. Share their responses as a group. Possible questions include:

• How does video conferencing work?
• What are the features of the software program they use?
• What are the benefits of video conferencing?

Students can then work in small groups to determine and jot important questions and related information in the main body of text in "Keypals."

This strategy of question and answer outlining is an effective way for students to organize information for comprehension and study purposes. Provide the students with an opportunity to put this skill into use in future reading in any curricular areas.

Writing

Create Images

Have the students consider the effectiveness of the phrase Morgan added to her poem when Lyle asked her to describe the mountain more vividly. Ask them to describe the picture that comes to their minds with the phrase "top of the mountain," and then "mountains stand higher than the clouds." Discuss how their images are enriched by the second phrase.

Provide the students with simple phrases, such as the following, and together brainstorm a variety of image-producing phrases to expand what is given.
– by the creek
– frost on the trees
– leaves on the ground

leaves on the ground
– a crunching, crackling sound under my feet
– a carpet of fall colors
– mounds of carefully raked leaves
– stepping on soggy, wet leaves after the rain

To help the students fully appreciate the different images well-crafted phrases can produce, ask each one to choose one of the brainstormed phrases and sketch the image that it produced in their minds. Students who illustrated phrases built around the same original one can then get together in a group and share their images.

Have the students look at pieces of their own writing with a partner to find and discuss:
• image producing phrases they have included
• revisions they could make to include imagery or more precise imagery

Encourage the students to watch for possibilities for image-producing descriptions when revising their writing over the next while.

Oral Communication

Participate in an Editing Conference

Talk with the students about the role of the editor and the writer in an editing conference. Together create a chart, listing both of their responsibilities with regards to the writing and to editing each other.

Roles in an Editing Conference

As the Editor ...
- read the piece of writing over carefully and think about it
- tell what things you like about the piece
- only look at a few features of the writing at each session
- first, consider what the writer is trying to say in the writing—is it clear?
- check to see if things flow well and follow a logical order—is anything missing?
- ask questions and make suggestions, but without being critical
- give the writer a chance to think about what you've said or asked
- let the writer ask questions
- look at things like vocabulary and sentence structure in following sessions
- look at things like punctuation, spelling, and grammar in final sessions

As the Writer ...
- put your best effort into the draft to be brought to the editing session
- listen carefully to the editor's suggestions
- ask questions to help you understand what the editor means
- think about the editor's suggestions
- decide which changes to make in your writing
- revise your writing and read it over
- make any other changes you think will improve your writing and bring this draft to your next editing session

Have the students work in pairs to hold a series of editing conferences about recent pieces of their writing, alternating the roles of editor and writer.

 Assessment See **Assess Learning**, page 67.

LINK TO CURRICULUM

Language Arts

Write a Keypal or Penpal

As a class or individual activity, the students can find and correspond with a keypal or penpal in another province or country. Encourage them to make a bulletin board display where they can share what they learn about the home area of their keypals or penpals. Or, they could form discussion groups where they talk about interesting things they find out.

  By visiting the World Surfari Web page at **http://www.supersurf.com** students can talk or leave messages for kids around the world.

For free service to help teachers and classes link with partners in other countries and cultures for e-mail classroom penpal and project exchange, enter the Schoolnet—Intercultural E-Mail Classroom connection at: **http://www.stolaf.edu/ network/iecc/**

Science

Write an Animal Report

Invite the students to think of an animal in their area or in Canada that they think would be of interest to a keypal or penpal in another country. They can prepare a report, complete with pictures and headings, to provide information about that animal. The reports can be compiled into a booklet and sent to a student or class in another country.

Students can use an encyclopedia CD-ROM as a source of information about their chosen animal. (See pages 5 and (ii) for resource information.)

Technology

Explore Communication Technology

Interested students can work together to find someone who is knowledgeable about a communication technology they are interested in, and arrange for that person to visit them in class and teach them how it works and/or how to use it.

Social Studies

Set Up an Information Corner

Students, in small groups, can select a country of interest and gather books, Internet printouts, pictures, and other informational materials about that country. Each group can then arrange the material in an attractive display in an information corner, and other members of the class can browse through it at various times to pick up bits of information about the different countries.

Learn About Folk Festivals

Students can reread the message from an Australian keypal about the Port Fairy Folk Festival, then think of folk festivals they know about. They can check the Internet, tourist bureaus, music organizations, local newspapers and agencies, and so on to find out about local or other folk festivals and make advertising pamphlets telling about them.

Oral Communication (see p. 64)

At different times in their peer editing, students can do a **self-assessment** of their performance in the role of editor and/or writer. A checklist developed from the student-generated chart could be used. The checklist could be adapted for **peer assessment.**

	Yes	Not this time
As the editor, I: – read and thought about the writing		
– told what I like		
– chose a few features to look at		
– thought about the writer's ideas first		
– checked the flow and order of things		
– asked questions and made suggestions without being critical		
– gave the writer a chance to think about what I said or asked		
– let the writer ask questions		
– looked at vocabulary, sentences, punctuation, ... in later sessions		
As the writer, I: – put my best effort into the writing		
– listened carefully to the editor's suggestions		
– asked questions to help clarify what the editor meant		
– thought about the editor's suggestions		
– decided which changes to make		
– revised my writing and read it over		
– made any other changes I thought would improve my writing		

Fax Facts

In this short story by E. M. Hunnicutt, Barney experiences conflict between exploring a multitude of uses for the family's new fax machine and spending time learning the words for a new song with his band. The incidents are humorous, but at the same time, there are a few lessons to be learned as well.

Anthology, pages 45-48   Blackline Masters 10,11, and 25
Learning Strategy Card 45

Learning Choices

LINK TO EXPERIENCE

Learn About the Fax Machine

Talk About Being Preocccupied

READ AND RESPOND TO TEXT

READING FOCUS

* read a variety of fiction and non-fiction materials for different purposes

  Assessment
* STRATEGY: **follow along**

REVISIT THE TEXT

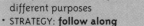

READING
Read for the Moral or Lesson
* explain their interpretation of a written work, supporting it with evidence from the work and from their own knowledge and experience

  Assessment

WRITING
Language Workshop — Grammar
* use correctly the conventions of grammar (sentence fragments)
Language Workshop — Spelling
* plurals; soft "c" pattern; /īze/ sound

ORAL COMMUNICATION
Read Orally with Expression
* use tone of voice and gestures to enhance the message and help convince or persuade listeners in conversations, discussions, or presentations

LINK TO CURRICULUM

LANGUAGE ARTS
Write a Story with a Lesson

LANGUAGE ARTS/THE ARTS
Draw a Cartoon Strip

THE ARTS
Hold a Sing-Along

SOCIAL STUDIES
Discuss Interpersonal Relationships and Technology

Key Learning Expectations

Students will
* read a variety of fiction and non-fiction materials for different purposes **(Reading Focus, p. 69)**
* explain their interpretation of a written work, supporting it with evidence from the work and from their own knowledge and experience **(Reading Mini Lesson, p. 70)**
* use correctly the conventions of grammar (sentence fragments) **(Writing Mini Lesson, p. 70)**
* use tone of voice and gestures to enhance the message and help convince or persuade listeners in conversations, discussions, or presentations **(Oral Communication Mini Lesson, p. 72)**

LINK TO EXPERIENCE

Learn About the Fax Machine

Invite someone into the classroom to talk about fax machines, the way they operate, and special features some may have. Encourage students to ask questions, and if at all possible, provide them with opportunities to use a fax machine.

Or, arrange for the students to watch your school's fax machine in action and talk to the person who operates it most frequently.

Or, discuss fax machines with the students, asking them to share what they know. Provide any information you can about fax machines.

Talk About Being Preoccupied

Write the word "preoccupied" on the board and, with the students, discuss its meaning. Ask students to tell about situations in which they or someone they know was preoccupied with a particular thought or doing a particular thing. Discuss some of the problems that could arise as a result of this.

Sayings such as "a bee in your bonnet" or "a one track mind" are used to describe people who are preoccupied with something. You may want to discuss these and others with your students.

READ AND RESPOND TO TEXT

Reading Focus

Blackline Master 10

Use a **follow along** strategy. Students can read the story independently, using Blackline Master 10 as a guide. Have them jot their responses to the questions on the blackline master and then share them with a partner.

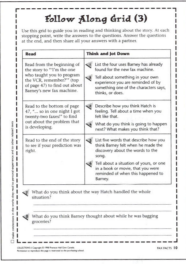

Follow Along Grid (3)

Use this grid to guide you in reading and thinking about the story. At each stopping point, write the answers to the questions. Answer the questions at the end, and then share all your answers with a partner.

Read	Think and Jot Down
Read from the beginning of the story to "I'm the one who taught you to program the VCR, remember?" (top of page 47) to find out about Barney's new fax machine.	List the four uses Barney has already found for the new fax machine. / Tell about something in your own experience you are reminded of by something one of the characters says, thinks, or does.
Read to the bottom of page 47, "... so in one night I got twenty-two faxes!" to find out about the problem that is developing.	Describe how you think Hatch is feeling. Tell about a time when you felt like that. / What do you think is going to happen next? What makes you think that?
Read to the end of the story to see if your prediction was right.	List five words that describe how you think Barney felt when he made the discovery about the words to the song. / Tell about a situation of yours, or one in a book or movie, that you were reminded of when this happened to Barney.

What do you think about the way Hatch handled the whole situation?

What do you think Barney thought about while he was bagging groceries?

COLLECTIONS © Copyright © 1998 Prentice Hall Ginn Canada. Permission to reproduce this page is restricted to the purchasing school.   FAX FACTS **10**

Blackline Master 10

Reader Response

Students could
- hold a conversation about the story to discuss questions such as:
  - **Why did Barney ask for faxes about sheep farms, menus, and weather reports? What does this tell you about him?**
  - **Did you think the story was funny or interesting? Why or why not?**
  - **What happened in the story to show you that Hatch knew Barney well?**
  - **What would you have done if you were Barney's dad? Hatch?**
  - **Have you ever been preoccupied with one thing? What happened?**
- check their list of uses of a fax machine they generated to see how many were included in the story and add any missing ones.
- write a description of the band Barney plays in.
- find the colloquial or slang expressions in the story and jot them in their journals.
- in small groups, talk about parts of the story they found humorous, explaining why they found them funny.
- make a story map, including the problem/solution of the plot.

Assessment See **Assess Learning**, page 74.

Get Ready to Read

Invite the students to brainstorm as many specific uses as they can think of for the fax machine. List these on the board. After reading the selection, they can see how many of their ideas were included in the story.

REVISIT THE TEXT

Reading

Read for the Moral or Lesson

First, guide the students in assessing Barney's various thoughts and actions by discussing questions such as the following:
- Did Barney's actions impact on others? In what way?
- Did Barney have good intentions in the story? Did he follow through with his intentions?
- Was Barney realistic in his thinking about being able to learn the words to the song?
- Did Barney think about the possible consequences of his actions?
- Did Barney try to remedy the situation? Was his idea a good one?
- Did he or anyone else do anything dishonest?

Then, have the students suggest what they think Barney learned from this experience. Together, write a sentence(s) summarizing the moral(s) of the story or lesson(s) they think Barney learned. Discuss too, whether they think anyone else in the story learned a lesson and what it was.

In small groups, ask the students to share stories they have read that have a moral or lesson. Encourage them to go beyond the traditional lesson tales by thinking about short stories and novels. Then have them choose one or two stories and write a summary statement of the lesson or moral on file cards, along with the title. The cards could be posted on the bulletin board, and students who have read the same stories can discuss whether or not they agree with the lesson/moral.

Writing

Language Workshop — Grammar

Blackline Master 11

Review with the students complete sentences and sentence fragments, using examples from the story.

Ask the students which of the examples express a complete thought—have both a subject and predicate, and which are sentence fragments. Some students may need guidance to recognize that "Come here!" and other command sentences are complete because the subject is understood or implied.

ONGOING ASSESSMENT

Consider:
- ☐ Are the students able to recognize stories that have a lesson or moral?
- ☐ Can the students articulate/summarize the moral or lesson of a story they have read?

- Doing that silly jig to her music.
- It was a junk fax.
- I tried to keep out of Hatch's way so he wouldn't ask questions.
- An advertisement someone sends you without asking.
- Come here!

Have the students look through "Fax Facts" to find examples of sentences that are not complete thoughts and read them aloud in the context of a few other sentences around them. Note that what they find are all examples of sentence fragments used in dialogue. Discuss why the author probably chose to use sentence fragments and how they add to the story.

For practice in identifying sentence fragments and in using them effectively in dialogue, the students could complete Blackline Master 11, *Sentence Fragments*.

Many writers use sentence fragments, especially in dialogue, because that is how people often talk.

Blackline Master 11

Language Workshop — Spelling
• plurals; soft "c" pattern; /ī ze/ sound

Blackline Master 25

Explore and Discover

Use Blackline Master 25 and the **sort, share, discuss,** and **chart** procedure outlined on page 17 to work with the words.

In discussing the words, have students note the soft "c" words and recall which letters control the /c/ sound. Make a chart listing the plural words according to the way in which the plurals have been formed, adding others they know how to spell. Look at the three words with the /ī ze/ sound, noting the two spellings. List other words under either "ize" or "ise," checking in a dictionary for the correct spelling. Have students form a generalization.

"ize" words	"ise" words
memorize	advertisement/advertise
glamorize	televise
realize/realization	advise
recognize	
organize/organization	

Follow this exploration with a **pretest, study and practise,** and a **post test** as outlined on page 17.

With a few exceptions, generally Canadian spellings are "ize." In countries such as Great Britain, Australia, and New Zealand, the "ise" spelling is used.

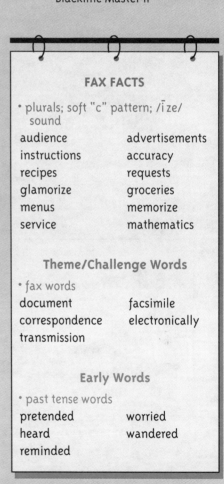

FAX FACTS

• plurals; soft "c" pattern; /ī ze/ sound

audience	advertisements
instructions	accuracy
recipes	requests
glamorize	groceries
menus	memorize
service	mathematics

Theme/Challenge Words

• fax words

document	facsimile
correspondence	electronically
transmission	

Early Words

• past tense words

pretended	worried
heard	wandered
reminded	

There is more than one accepted pronunciation of "advertisement." Challenge students to look up the pronunciations in a dictionary and share their findings.

Study and Practise

Students could
- use Learning Strategy Card 4 to study words identified after the pretest.
- set their word cards out in a row from easiest to most difficult. They then choose the five most difficult words, write them out twice, and use them in sentences.
- make a word animal by writing words to create the body, legs, head, ... of an imaginary animal.

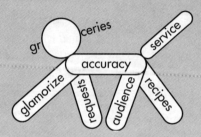

Oral Communication

Read Orally with Expression

Choose a part of the story that could be read aloud expressively, preferably one that includes dialogue. Ask the students to first read the passage silently and consider how it would be most effectively read aloud. Together, list clues from the story that would help them determine the most effective way to read the passage. They should look for such things as:

- punctuation
- what has gone on before
- which character(s) is involved
- words that describe how a character is speaking
- words that describe what the situation is like or how people are feeling
- places where gestures could be used to add to the reading

Invite volunteers to read the selected passage. Discuss each reader's use of pitch, pace, tone, and expressive gestures, noting what was particularly effective and offering suggestions for improvement.

Have the students select another passage from this story or from another one they have read to read aloud to a partner. Ask the partners to select aspects of the reading that were most effective and make suggestions for ways in which the oral reading might be improved.

LINK TO CURRICULUM

Language Arts

Write a Story with a Lesson

Interested students could write short stories with a lesson. They may wish to make them humorous, like "Fax Facts." After they have revised and edited their work, possibly making use of computer technology, they could bind their stories to make a book to lend to another class.

Language Arts/The Arts

Draw a Cartoon Strip

Students could choose a part of the story to "tell" in a cartoon strip. Or, a group of students could work together to plan and draw the complete story as a comic book. Others might like to create a strip showing what Barney thought about while he was bagging groceries.

The Arts

Hold a Sing-Along

Students can work together to prepare for an old-fashioned sing-a-long. As a group, they can decide on who to invite, where to hold it, what type of songs to sing, and so on. They might consider holding one for seniors or for young children.

Suggest that they assign different tasks to group members—selecting songs, getting the musical accompaniment, writing out the words, making advertising posters, ...

Social Studies

Discuss Interpersonal Relationships and Technology

In small groups, the students can talk about the positive and negative effects technology, such as television, computers, fax machines, telephone answering machines, ..., have on the way people relate to one another. Suggest that they jot the main conclusions of and/or ideas arising from their discussions on chart paper and post them so others can read them.

Assessment

A s s e s s   L e a r n i n g

Reader Response (see p. 69)

Learning Strategy Card 45

Students could read Learning Strategy Card 45 and use the information to choose a way to **self-assess** the response activity they chose.

OR

You may wish to assess the response activities that the students chose. To prepare for the assessment, students could complete a **self-assessment** using the *Reader Response Activity Sheet* from the *COLLECTIONS 6 Assessment Handbook*.

OR

You might prefer to ask all students to write answers to the questions in "hold a conversation" about the selection. Use the written answers as a **work sample** assignment or test of how well the students understood and could relate to the selection.

Note: With some students, you may prefer to hold individual conferences so they can respond orally to the questions.

In Your Face

This article by Elizabeth MacLeod explains how morphing and digital warping programs and other high-tech computer programs can change and project facial appearances for a variety of purposes.

Anthology, pages 49-52
Learning Strategy Card 46

Blackline Masters 12 and 25

Key Learning Expectations

Students will
• summarize and explain the main ideas in information materials, and cite details that support the main ideas **(Reading Focus, p. 76)**
• read a variety of fiction and non-fiction materials for different purposes **(Reading Mini Lesson, p. 77)**
• select words and expressions to create specific effects **(Writing Mini Lesson, p. 78)**
• communicate a main idea about a topic and describe a sequence of events **(Oral Communication Mini Lesson, p. 79)**

LINK TO EXPERIENCE

Explore Distortions

Bring in a large magnifying mirror or a piece of shiny tin and have the students view themselves and talk about what happens to their image. Invite them to tell about other ways of creating facial or body distortions, such as the fun-mirrors at fairs, looking at a person up close through binoculars, looking at your hand under rippling water, and so on.

Tell About Special Effect Distortions

Ask the students to tell about movies or cartoons in which a character's facial expressions or whole bodies have been distorted to create special effects. Ask them to describe the weird faces and body shapes and discuss how they think the animators created these effects.

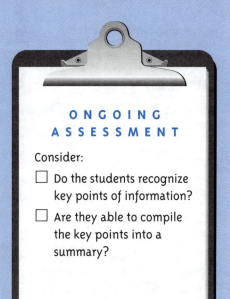

Reading Focus

Students can use an adaptation of the **read and summarize** strategy. First, ask them to scan the article and write the headings on a piece of paper, leaving room beneath each heading for notes. Then give each student some small self-stick notes.

Ask the students to read the article and jot down brief notations of important points in each section, one point per note, and stick the notes under the appropriate heading.

After reading the whole article, have the students read over their notes to review the information. Encourage them to reread sections to clarify or gain more information, if necessary. Then have them order the notes within each section and use these as a guide to write section summaries.

In pairs, the students can select two of their summaries, read them to one another, and compare what information they considered important.

Reader Response

Students could
- refer to a dictionary to find the word that "morph" was made from and talk about what the original word has to do with morphing.
- list and categorize as many uses they can think of for the way computers can age, change, morph, or rearrange faces and whole bodies.
- talk about why morphing is used in movies, cartoons, and commercials.
- with a small group, collect and display cartoons, advertisements, story illustrations, caricatures, ... that show changes, projections, and distortions.
- write a description of a person's face, first in general terms, and then with details.
- find both a photo and a computer drawn picture of a person (possibly a movie actor) and compare the two.
- discuss how they might make use of computer morphing and digital warping programs.

REVISIT THE TEXT

Reading

Look at Unity and Coherence in a Paragraph

Read aloud the paragraph under "Place That Face," while students follow along to identify the sentence(s) that contains the main idea of the paragraph. Focus on the other sentences and discuss whether/how they develop or expand on the main idea. Then, talk about how the ideas in the paragraph seem to fit with one another and are arranged in an order that makes the information easy to understand.

Ask the students to look for words or phrases that help to develop the unity and coherence of the paragraph, such as " When," "That's why," "This way," "So," "the next time."

Have students work on their own to analyze another paragraph from the selection. Then talk about what they found: the sentence(s) that expressed the main idea of the paragraph, whether all sentences were focused on the main idea, whether there was a smooth flow of ideas, and words that help with unity and coherence.

Make a chart with words and phrases from this selection that assist in creating unity and coherence in paragraphs. This chart can be added to from time to time.

> The sentence(s) that expresses the main idea of a paragraph is called the **topic sentence.** The other sentences that tell more about the main idea are called **detail sentences.**

> A good paragraph has
> • a main idea expressed in one or more sentences
> • unity—all sentences are focused on the main idea
> • coherence—smooth connections between the sentences and a logical order of sentences

Words and Phrases for Creating Unity and Coherence

- When
- That's why
- This way
- So, the next time
- In the future
- First
- Then
- In seconds

Discuss with the students how looking for unity and coherence in a paragraph can help them understand what they are reading. Stress the importance, also, of these features being included in their own writing. You may wish to ask the students to select a topic of interest or one related to another curricular area and write a paragraph with a main idea, unity, and coherence.

Writing

Write Catchy Sentences

On the board or overhead, write examples, such as the following, to illustrate catchy sentences that give the article an interesting style:

– Let's face it— your face is more than just a place for your nose, eyes, and mouth.

– "Hey, that's the guy on TV!"

– Want to know what you'll look like in a few years?

– Why? Because they know those are the areas people really look at when they look at faces.

Have the students skim through the article to find these sentences and read them aloud in the context of a few other sentences. Discuss the catchy sentence patterns: why they are effective as individual sentences and how they add to the article as a whole. Have them find other catchy sentences in this article or other text and list these on the board or overhead as well.

When they have a "feel" for what makes a catchy sentence, they can look through pieces of their own writing for sentences that can be changed to provide interest and variety in their writing. Allow time for pairs or small groups to share both their original writing and their revised, catchy sentences and phrases with others.

IN YOUR FACE

• ure, al, ic patterns

facial	structure	features
electronics	criminal	physical
measurement	realistic	digital
future	creatures	specific

Theme/Challenge Words

• digital art words

morphing	distortion
animators	warping
reconstruction	

Early Words

• -ly pattern

early	actually
quickly	probably
amazingly	

Language Workshop — Spelling
• ure, al, ic patterns

Blackline Master 25

Explore and Discover

Use Blackline Master 25 and the **sort, share, discuss,** and **chart** procedure outlined on page 17 to work with the words.

In discussing the words, have the students identify spelling patterns in the list words; "ment" can be included along with the more frequent "ure," "al," and "ic." Write these patterns as headings on the board and ask volunteers to list spelling words under the appropriate heading. Small groups of students can then take one pattern and make a chart-sized word web with words from the list and others they know with the same pattern.

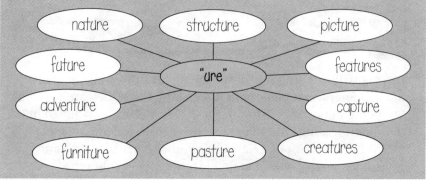

Follow this exploration with a **pretest, study and practise,** and a **post test** as outlined on page 17.

<u>Study and Practise</u>

Students could
- use Learning Strategy Card 4 to study words identified after the pretest.
- on the front of their word cards, trace over the letters of the patterns "ure," "ic," "al" in three different colors.
- make a matrix with the number of syllables and spelling patterns, using words from the list and others they know.

	"ic" pattern	"ure" pattern	"al" pattern
2 syllables	picnic	structure features creatures future	facial
3 syllables	specific fantastic	measurement	digital criminal physical
4 syllables	electronics realistic	temperature	

Oral Communication

Give a Speech

mini LESSON

Blackline Master 12
Learning Strategy Card 46

Refer students to the statement about computers in the deck (near the title) of the article: "They're high-tech masters... ." Discuss what is meant by the term "high-tech masters" and have the students brainstorm a wide range of things computers can do. Choose one of these functions as the basis for a speech that will provide information about such things as how the function works, why it is useful, and what it may be used for in the future.

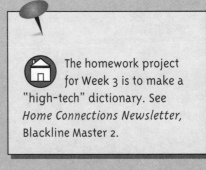

The homework project for Week 3 is to make a "high-tech" dictionary. See *Home Connections Newsletter,* Blackline Master 2.

Encourage the students to use appropriate vocabulary they know/have learned when talking about computers and what they can do.

First, read Learning Strategy Card 46 with the students. Then make a class chart of things to know and think about when preparing a speech.

Preparing a Speech

Know your audience
– What will make the topic interesting for them?
– How much do they likely know about the topic?

Know the purpose of your speech
– Why is the topic important?

Know your topic
– Will you need to do some research?
– What sources will you use?

Know the organization of your speech
– Will you organize it by sub-topics? chronological order? questions? ...?

Know how to begin and end it effectively
– Will you start with a story? question? statement? ...?
– Will you end with a summary statement? story? joke? moral? ...?

Know where to add gestures, charts, or illustrations
– What points can be emphasized with gestures?
– What can be more clearly explained with charts or illustrations?

<aside>
In all oral presentations, good planning is necessary. But speakers often deviate from their plans depending on the reaction of the audiences. Also, sometimes speakers miss a point in their presentations and need to make adjustments to accommodate this. Students should be made aware that the ability to make changes increases with practice in public speaking, and that a thorough knowledge of the subject is the key to being able to make these changes.
</aside>

Then, plan the speech around these considerations. Make an overhead transparency of Blackline Master 12, *Talk It Up*, as a framework within which to plan. Once the speech is planned, a volunteer or volunteers could practise and give it to the class.

Provide students with their own copies of the blackline master to use in planning a speech on a topic of their own choosing, perhaps one related to their social studies or science curriculum. Encourage them to review their plans with a partner and make any additions or changes after the discussion. The reverse side of the planning sheet can be used to create an outline for the talk.

Blackline Master 12

Provide opportunities for the students to practise their speech and give it to a small group or to the class.

 Assessment See **Assess Learning**, page 82.

INK TO CURRICULUM

Language Arts

Write a Limerick

Students can write a humorous limerick that focuses on an exaggerated feature of an imaginary person. The limericks can be illustrated using a digital morphing program or by drawing a caricature.

Limerick format consists of a couplet and a triplet in an a-a-b-b-a arrangement.

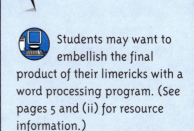

Students may want to embellish the final product of their limericks with a word processing program. (See pages 5 and (ii) for resource information.)

There was a young lad from St. Joe's
Who had a great humongous nose.
When he had to sniff
We all wondered if
We'd survive the horrendous blows.

Play an Identification Game

Interested students could work together to organize an identification game. They would need large photographs of people that could be easily seen by a group, or they could use short clips of people on video tape. They then show the photographs or clips briefly, one at a time, to a group of players. The players write down all the things they can remember about the person, or draw what they saw, and compare their responses before looking at the photo or video again.

The Arts

Age or Morph a Character

Interested students could find a magazine picture of a person's face that is approximately 10 cm by 12 cm in size. Have them cut the picture vertically in half and paste one side of the face onto a piece of drawing paper, leaving one half of the page free for them to draw an aged or morphed version of the face. The drawings could be colored to match the original picture, then the completed picture displayed on the bulletin board.

Science

Learn About the Face

Students can reread the information in the selection about the face and use the list as a starting point for researching the face. They might like to work with a partner or small group to make an illustrated fact sheet or booklet about the face: its muscles, skin, bones, and organs, what happens to different parts of the face as a person ages/grows, interesting trivia (how many muscles it takes to smile, frown), and so on.

 Assessment

A s s e s s   L e a r n i n g

Oral Communication (see p. 79)

Assessment here can be two-fold: using Blackline Master 12 as a **work sample** to indicate the student's planning, and listening to the speech and taking **anecdotal notes** about the content and presentation. For content, comment on such things as:
• choice of topic
• how well the student kept on topic
• appropriate and effective introduction and closing
• whether important points and supporting details were covered

For presentation, comment on such elements as:
• flow and organization of information
• clarity of information
• use of gestures, charts, illustrations

Peer or self-assessment is also an option, using much the same procedure.

Meet Emily of New Moon

In this interview, Catherine Rondina talks to twelve-year-old Martha MacIsaac from Charlottetown, P.E.I. Martha tells of her experiences and daily routine as the star of the television series, *Emily of New Moon*.

Anthology, pages 53-57   **Learning Strategy Cards 47 and 48**

Learning Choices

LINK TO EXPERIENCE

Talk About Famous Young People

Identify with a Movie/TV Character

READ AND RESPOND TO TEXT

READING FOCUS
• explain their interpretation of a written work, supporting it with evidence from the work and from their own knowledge and experience
• STRATEGY: **read and connect**

REVISIT THE TEXT

READING
Categorize and Summarize Biographical Information
• summarize and explain the main ideas in information materials, and cite details that support the main ideas

WRITING
Write an Interview
• communicate ideas and information for a variety of purposes and to specific audiences

ORAL COMMUNICATION
Memorize Lines
• communicate a main idea about a topic and describe a sequence of events

LINK TO CURRICULUM

LANGUAGE ARTS
Make a Book Collection

Create a Commercial

LANGUAGE ARTS/THE ARTS
Compare a Book and Movie

SOCIAL STUDIES
Learn About Prince Edward Island

SOCIAL STUDIES/MATHEMATICS
Create a Game

Key Learning Expectations

Students will
• explain their interpretation of a written work, supporting it with evidence from the work and from their own knowledge and experience (**Reading Focus, p. 84**)
• summarize and explain the main ideas in information materials, and cite details that support the main ideas (**Reading Mini Lesson, p. 85**)
• communicate ideas and information for a variety of purposes and to specific audiences (**Writing Mini Lesson, p. 86**)
• communicate a main idea about a topic and describe a sequence of events (**Oral Communication Mini Lesson, p. 86**)

LINK TO EXPERIENCE

Talk About Famous Young People

Ask the students to share what they know about young people who have become well known for their accomplishments in music, art, sports, movies, the circus, as a crusader, ... Discuss how their lives would be different from the lives of students in the class.

> The article "Free the Children!" in the *Looking for Answers* unit, is about Craig Kielburger, a 12-year-old child rights crusader.

Identify with a Movie/ TV Character

Ask the students to think about a young movie/TV character they would like to play. They can write about playing this character in their journals, telling why they would like to play that part, how they are suited for the role, what things they'd have to learn to do, and so on. They can share their thoughts with a small group or partner, if they wish.

ONGOING ASSESSMENT

Consider:

☐ Can the students relate in some way to the life Martha leads?

☐ Do the students acknowledge the challenges, responsibilities, and sacrifices involved in Martha's life?

To gather information about Lucy Maud Montgomery, students can follow the biographical charting used in the reading mini lesson on page 85.

Reading Focus

Students can use a **read and connect** strategy to learn about Martha MacIsaac and relate to her experiences. As they read the interview independently, ask them to jot five things they learn about Martha and note something that they were particularly interested in or could relate to personally. Ask them to also jot any connections they see in this article to other articles/stories they have read.

The students can share their jot notes in small groups.

Reader Response

Students could

• hold a conversation about the interview to discuss questions such as:

  – **How does Martha feel about her present career and its future possibilities?**

  – **Why would the friendship between Martha and Jane Hennesey be so important to Martha?**

  – **Why are auditions important? What other things might a producer/director look at in addition to an audition?**

  – **Would you like to have a personal tutor? What would be the pros and cons of having a tutor?**

  – **What stories/books have you read that have been made into a movie or TV series?**

  – **What do you think it would be like to be a young movie star? Is this something you would like to be? Why or why not?**

• reread the interview with a partner, with one taking the part of Martha and the other, the interviewer.

• use print or electronic dictionaries and the text of the interview to define the movie terms, "episode," "stand-in," "takes," "cue," "professional" and others they can think of.

• learn about Lucy Maud Montgomery.

• chart a daily or weekly schedule for Martha while she is shooting, filling in times that are not indicated.

• 🎧 listen to the *COLLECTIONS* audio version of the interview, and note impressions and characteristics of Martha that aren't evident in the printed version.

Reading

Categorize and Summarize Biographical Information

Discuss with the students the purpose of this interview, bringing out that it provides information about the life of Martha MacIsaac as related to her role in *Emily of New Moon*. Talk about how the information gathered through the interview could be re-organized into categories and used for a biography about Martha. With the students, list headings that could be used to organize the information in a chart or web.

Have the students skim the interview to find information to go under the headings. As they skim, they may also find information they wish to include that will require new headings. Begin a chart or web together, and have students complete it on their own.

Name: <u>Martha MacIsaac</u>

Age or Birthdate: <u>12 years</u>   Home or Birthplace: <u>Charlottetown, P.E.I.</u>

Personal Qualities	Education	Previous Experiences	Present Activities/ Career	Future
– confident – natural actress – friendly – good memory	– in grade 7 when started with Emily – is tutored while shooting movie	– in "Anne of Green Gables" after grade 5	–	–

Other Important Information:

Work with the students to underline key information and important details, and use them to write a short biography of the life of Martha as Emily Starr.

Interested students can choose a person of interest and gather information about his/her life, using a similar chart or web procedure. Information from a variety of print or electronic sources can be included. After selecting important information, they could write a biography that summarizes the information about that person, including pictures if possible. The biographies can be read to other students in small groups or compiled into a class booklet.

 Assessment   See **Assess Learning**, page 89.

Writing

Write an Interview

Learning Strategy Card 47

Talk with students about the format used for recording the interview:
- the speaker's initials of CR and MM
- the use of colons
- the lack of quotation marks

The format used here is common in text such as plays, interviews, and court testimony, where conversation is recorded. Another example appears in the first part of the selection "World Shrinkers."

Discuss why this format is appropriate for an interview, and ask the students to recall other places where they have seen conversation written in this way.

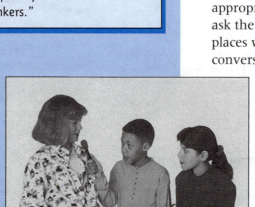

Have the students work in pairs to interview one another about some activity they are currently involved in and to record the interview following the pattern of "Meet Emily of New Moon." They may wish to tape-record the interviews, then transcribe them in the format. The written interviews could be posted for all the class to read.

For guidance and information about conducting an interview, students could read Learning Strategy Card 47.

Oral Communication

Memorize Lines

Learning Strategy Card 48

Have the students skim page 54 to find things that Martha mentions as being helpful to her for memorizing lines. Write these on the board or overhead. Invite the students to read Learning Strategy Card 48 and to use ideas from the card and others they can think of to add other tips to the chart.

Tips for Memorizing a Script

- get other actors to go over the scene with you a few times (Martha)
- have someone ready to cue you if you forget a line (Martha)
- understand the story so you know how it goes
- visualize the scene, action, and story
- know how you fit into the scene
- don't just cue yourself to a word or line of the speaker before you, because that person might make a mistake
- always pay attention to what is going on in the scene on stage
- practise until you are sure you know the lines
- practise whole scenes or chunks of lines with others, not just your own lines
- get ideas from others about how they remember lines

In small groups, students can select short plays, or scenes from longer ones, choose characters, directors, and prompters, and work together to memorize the script. After sufficient practise time, groups can perform these plays for others as a readers' theatre performance, but without the scripts.

LINK TO CURRICULUM

Language Arts

Make a Book Collection

Students can gather books written by Lucy Maud Montgomery and display them in the classroom library. They can set up a borrowing system so that students can read, review, and recommend favorite books.

The display can be enhanced with students' illustrations of favorite parts of books. Some may wish to audio-tape favorite parts for their classmates to listen to, or work with others to dramatize a chapter from one of the books.

Interested students may want to visit L. M. Montgomery's home page on the Internet to learn more about this author:
http://www.unl.edu/lucymaud/Montgomery/montgomery.htm

BOOKS BY LUCY MAUD MONTGOMERY

Anne of Ingleside. McClelland & Stewart.

Anne of Windy Willows. McClelland & Stewart.

Anne's House of Dreams. McClelland & Stewart.

Chronicles of Avonlea. McGraw-Hill Ryerson.

Emily's Quest. McClelland & Stewart.

The Golden Road. McGraw-Hill Ryerson.

Jane of Lantern Hill. McClelland & Stewart.

Students could use a storyboard to plan the commercial. This would help ensure a logical flow to the project. Also, the storyboard could be used to assess the activity if it was only taken to the planning stage.

Software such as *Adventure Canada* may help students research needed information for their television commercial. (See pages 5 and (ii) for resource information.)

Create a Commercial

In pairs or small groups, students can plan and enact a television commercial encouraging people to visit their part of Canada. In their planning, the students will need to consider what will make people want to visit and how they are going to catch viewers' attention (catchy phrases, tunes, actions, ...). Suggest that they watch television for examples of ads of this nature for other ideas.

 If possible, the commercial could be video-taped and shared with classmates, other classes, and families.

Language Arts/The Arts

Compare a Book and Movie

Provide the students with an opportunity to experience both the book and movie versions of a story, or have them recall ones they've read and viewed on their own. They can then make a chart or Venn Diagram showing the similarities and differences, and talk about their preferences and reasons for liking one better than the other with a partner or small group.

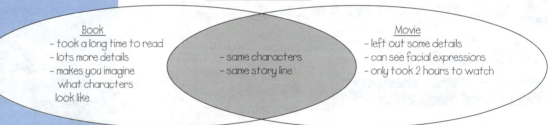

Sarah Plain and Tall

Book
- took a long time to read
- lots more details
- makes you imagine what characters look like

- same characters
- same story line

Movie
- left out some details
- can see facial expressions
- only took 2 hours to watch

Social Studies

Learn About Prince Edward Island

Interested students can learn about the province of Prince Edward Island, with a special emphasis on Charlottetown and Summerside. They might also want to find out about the Confederation Bridge.

Students could use books from the library and the Internet for the home page of Prince Edward Island. They could also fax or write the Tourism Board of Prince Edward Island and request material. Software such as *Adventure Canada* and *Canadian Encyclopedia* offer excellent information as well. (See pages 5 and (ii) for resource information.)

Students' findings could be recorded on an illustrated map with bits of information printed around the edges, or in another way of their own choosing.

Social Studies/Mathematics

Create a Game

Students can make question-and-answer cards using information from the interview and from other related reading and research. The questions could be about the life of Lucy Maud Montgomery, her books, and Prince Edward Island. They can also create math questions based on the distances travelled by Martha and her family, and about times spent in travel, shooting the series, school work, ..., . Various gameboards can be fashioned by the students for use with these cards.

Assess Learning

Reading (see p. 85)

Student's research charts or webs and biographies can be handed in as a **work sample** demonstrating their ability to gather, organize, and summarize information from text. In **assessing** their work, look for things such as the following:
- appropriate headings chosen
- information noted under correct headings
- key information and important details underlined
- biography summarizes important information in the chart or web

THEME: COMMUNICATING THROUGH MASS MEDIA

Anthology, pages 58-59

> **Fax Facts** — *a limerick*
>
> **Ways to Communicate** — *an acrostic poem*
>
> **Log On** — *a short story*
>
> **Conflict Resolution** — *e-mail messages*
>
> **My Hobby** — *a personal narrative*

STUDENT WRITING

LINK TO THE THEME

After reading the selections with a partner, the students could

- write in their journals about which selection they preferred and why.
- discuss the similarities and differences among the pieces of writing.
- write a sentence or two about each selection, telling how each is related to the theme of communicating through mass media.

Pairs of students could form small groups to share their ideas.

LINK TO THE WRITING PROCESS

Write a Story in Letters

Invite the students to reread the e-mails in "Conflict Resolution" and guide them to realize that, although sent by computer, they are still personal and informal letters. They both have a greeting and a closing, and Jenna adds a post script with her P.S. The sentences are short and to the point, yet have a friendly tone.

Discuss also how the author used these letters to tell a story; that is, when you read them, you can tell who the characters are, what the problem was, and how the problem was solved.

Invite pairs of students to write a story in letter form. They can use two letters to tell their story, or more if they wish. The stories can be written as letters or as e-mail letters.

Language Workshop — Style

- select words and expressions to create specific effects

Blackline Master 13

Teach/Explore/Discover

Have the students reread the opening paragraph of "Log On," and note how the author opens his story and establishes the setting. Ask them to comment on the effectiveness of the opening, and what it tells them about the story to come.

Provide some other examples of attention-getting story openers, and have similar discussions about their effectiveness.

Jot generalizations about story openers that result from the discussion, for example:
A story opener can:
- introduce the character
- set the mood of the story
- give details about the setting and when the story is taking place
- give hints or clues about the story plot

Practise/Apply
Students could
- complete Blackline Master 13, *Interesting Ways To Begin*.
- revisit a piece of their writing to see if they can/should rewrite the beginning in a more interesting way.
- look through stories and novels they have read and find openers they like.

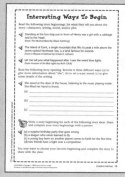

Blackline Master 13

LINK TO THE WRITER

Read Mark's comment, then have students talk about topics they have written on and why they chose them. They can also discuss
- their favorite topic to write about and why.
- a new topic they would like to write about.
- how they collect their ideas for writing about something
- two new things they could do to collect ideas and topics for future writing.

Anti-Snore Machine

This story, taken from *Ratbags and Rascals: Funny Stories* by Robin Klein, tells of the frustrated attempts of girls at a camp to do something about the incredible snoring of one of their cabin mates.

Anthology, pages 60-63
Learning Strategy Card 49

Blackline Masters 14 and 26

Learning Choices

LINK TO EXPERIENCE

Illustrate Camp or Holiday Stories

Dramatize Snoring Situations

READ AND RESPOND TO TEXT

READING FOCUS
• explain their interpretation of a written work, supporting it with evidence from the work and from their own knowledge and experience
• STRATEGY: **read and reflect**

REVISIT THE TEXT

READING
Explore Vocabulary
• understand the vocabulary and language structures (dictionary, thesaurus, and electronic media) appropriate for this grade level

WRITING
Language Workshop —
Punctuation
• use correctly the conventions of punctuation (dialogue)
Language Workshop — Spelling
• ly, ous patterns

VISUAL COMMUNICATION
Create a Flow Diagram
• create a variety of media works

LINK TO CURRICULUM

LANGUAGE ARTS
Write a Sequence Poem

LANGUAGE ARTS/THE ARTS
Perform a Readers' Theatre

HEALTH
Find Out About Snoring

SCIENCE/MATHEMATICS
Find Out About Noise Levels

Key Learning Expectations

Students will
• explain their interpretation of a written work, supporting it with evidence from the work and from their own knowledge and experience (**Reading Focus, p. 92**)
• understand the vocabulary and language structures (dictionary, thesaurus, and electronic media) appropriate for this grade level (**Reading Mini Lesson, p. 93**)
• use correctly the conventions of punctuation (dialogue) (**Writing Mini Lesson, p. 94**)
• create a variety of media works (**Visual Communication Mini Lesson, p. 97**)

LINK TO EXPERIENCE

Illustrate Camp or Holiday Stories

Ask a few students to tell about funny things that happened to them while camping/holidaying with a group, friends, or family. Then have each student illustrate a personal humorous experience or one that they know about in a cartoon strip or picture. The illustrations could be shared in small groups.

Dramatize Snoring Situations

In small groups, students can tell about and then act out situations involving snoring that they know about through experience, through the stories of others, or ones they make up. After each role play, they can talk about how the different people in the situation felt about what had gone on.

Reading Focus

Use a **read and reflect** strategy. The students can read the story independently, then make and fill in a story map, showing characters, setting, problem, events, and solution. Have them compare and discuss their completed maps with a partner.

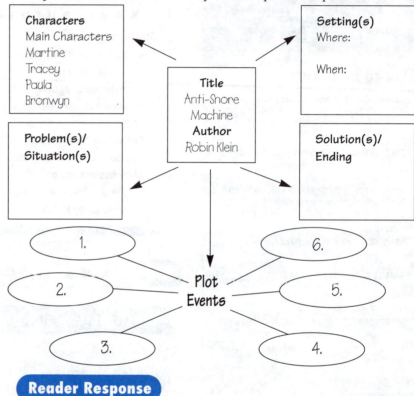

Characters
Main Characters
Martine
Tracey
Paula
Bronwyn

Setting(s)
Where:

When:

Title
Anti-Snore
Machine
Author
Robin Klein

Problem(s)/ Situation(s)

Solution(s)/ Ending

Plot Events

1.
2.
3.
4.
5.
6.

Reader Response

Students could
- hold a conversation about the story to discuss questions such as:
  - **How did the title fit with what you expected?**
  - **What did you think of Paula and Tracey's reason for wanting to be in the same room as Martine? Do you think Martine knew their reason?**
  - **Why didn't Paula and Tracey let Bronwyn make her suggestions?**
  - **What did you think of Paula's invention?**
  - **Why do you think turning Martine on her side worked?**
  - **How do you think Paula and Tracey felt after Bronwyn's suggestion worked?**
  - **Which of the characters do you relate to most closely in this story? Tell why.**
- read other stories from the book *Ratbags and Rascals.*
- list five things people tried to blot out or stop Martine's snoring.
- read aloud the passages that describe Martine's snoring, then write their own description of the sound of a person's snoring.

REVISIT THE TEXT

Reading

Explore Vocabulary

On the board, write words from the selection that the students might find unfamiliar in either meaning or pronunciation; for example: glucose, indulgently, sympathetic, weary, astonishing, belfry, understudies, complicated, poised, inflate, momentous, thwarted, exhaustion, and indignantly. Work as a group to model an exploration and charting approach to learn more about these words.

Have the students locate these words in the story and read aloud the sentences in which they appear. Together, talk about the pronunciation and meaning of the words, as determined in context. Then confirm/extend their ideas using a dictionary and thesaurus. Chart their ideas/responses.

Sentence/part of a sentence with word and meaning from context	Dictionary pronunciation and meaning that fits word as used in sentence	Synonyms from a Thesaurus
It looks very **complicated** – difficult, hard to do	**kom** pli kāt id – not easy to understand or do; intricate	– confusing – elaborate – muddled up
... and **poised** on one end will be a heavy object – balanced – positioned		

On their own, students can continue in this way with other unfamiliar words from the selection. To extend the activity, they could start a vocabulary booklet of unfamiliar vocabulary in other reading selections or curricular areas, using the chart idea or another format of their own choosing.

Students could refer to Learning Strategy Card 1 to review how to use a thesaurus.

Writing

Language Workshop — Punctuation

Blackline Master 14
Learning Strategy Card 49

On the board or overhead, write these examples of dialogue from the story and underline the exact words spoken:

1. Miss Lewis stopped calling out indulgently, "Girls, put the lights out now, please."
2. Everyone sat up in bed saying polite things such as, "I say, Martine, do you mind …"
3. "We couldn't get any sleep all night because of your snoring!" Tracey and Paula said.
4. "We can't go a whole week without sleep," Tracey said desperately.
5. "Much easier to— " said Bronwyn.
6. "Me neither," said Tracey. "Is there room for my things in your Mom's car?"

Have students look at the underlined parts and identify features of capitalization and punctuation in the dialogue. Help them in developing a reference chart for capitalization and punctuation in dialogue.

Read Learning Strategy Card 49 with the students to review how to write dialogue and to note rules about capitalization and punctuation in quotations to be included in the reference chart.

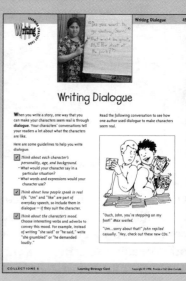

The term "speaker tag" refers to all the words that are not the exact words of the speaker—the words that tell who is speaking and how they are speaking.

Writing Dialogue

Capitals

• The first of the speaker's words begins with a capital.

Punctuation

• Quotation marks go around the exact words of a speaker, no matter where the quote is in the sentence.
• Punctuation marks at the end of a speaker's words come before the second set of quotation marks.
• If the speaker's words come at the beginning of the sentence, they end with a comma except when:
   – they are a question or an exclamation. Then they end with a question mark or an exclamation point.
   – they are interrupted. Then they end with a dash.
   – the speaker didn't finish what he/she was saying. Then they end with ellipsis points.
• If the speaker's words come at the end of a sentence, they end with the punctuation mark appropriate for the quote (period, exclamation point, question mark, ...)
• If the speaker tag is at the beginning of a sentence, it is separated from the quote by a comma.
• If the speaker tag is at the end of a sentence, it ends with a period.
• Speaker tags only need to be used once. If the speaker continues to talk after being identified, the dialogue is written with one set of quotation marks around it all.

For practise in writing dialogue using these conventions, the students can complete Blackline Master 14, *Writing Dialogue*.

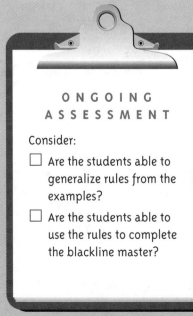

Blackline Master 14

Some students may be interested in knowing about single quotes. These are used to identify a quote within a quote. Or they are used to identify a name of something that would normally be in quotes, but is used in a quote. For example:
 – "The librarian said, 'You are making too much noise at the computers,' when we were trying to find a new website," Tony explained to his teacher.
 – Kristen said, "You should listen to the song 'Wacky Weekend.' It will fit in great with our skit."

ONGOING ASSESSMENT

Consider:

☐ Are the students able to generalize rules from the examples?

☐ Are the students able to use the rules to complete the blackline master?

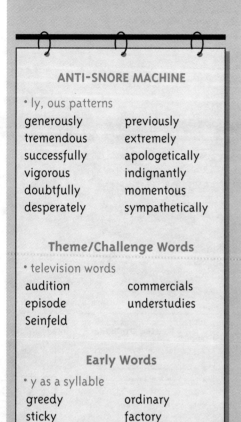

ANTI-SNORE MACHINE

• ly, ous patterns

generously	previously
tremendous	extremely
successfully	apologetically
vigorous	indignantly
doubtfully	momentous
desperately	sympathetically

Theme/Challenge Words

• television words

audition	commercials
episode	understudies
Seinfeld	

Early Words

• y as a syllable

greedy	ordinary
sticky	factory
weary	

Blackline Master 26

Explore and Discover

Use Blackline Master 26 and the **sort, share, discuss,** and **chart** procedure outlined on page 17 to work with the words.

In discussing the words, work with the students to create a Venn Diagram showing words with the "ly" and "ous" pattern and those with both.

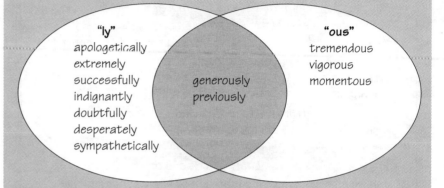

"ly"
apologetically
extremely
successfully
indignantly
doubtfully
desperately
sympathetically

generously
previously

"ous"
tremendous
vigorous
momentous

Follow this exploration with a **pretest, study and practise,** and a **post test** as outlined on page 17.

Study and Practise

Students could

• use Learning Strategy Card 4 to study words identified after the pretest.

• on the front of their word cards, draw curved lines under each of the syllables, consulting print or electronic dictionaries to ensure that they are correct. They then highlight the syllables that make any root words.

• write 5 sentences using their study words, trying to put at least two of their words into each sentence, and underlining those words.

Visual Communication

Create a Flow Diagram

Have students turn to page 62 and use their fingers to follow along on the diagram as you read aloud the paragraph giving Paula's explanation of how her machine works. Then talk with students about how the verbal cause and effect explanation and the pictorial flow match.

Ask the students to identify features in the diagram that assist the viewer in following the flow and to suggest other helpful features they think could be added to the diagram. List all these on the board or overhead:

Features of a Flow Diagram
- drawings of objects
- labels for objects
- arrows showing the direction of flow of events and movement of objects
- mark the beginning and end
- objects numbered in correct sequence
- title for diagram
- include a small picture showing the end result

Students can then plan an invention of their own. Have them make both a pictorial flow diagram, using the list of helpful features as a guide, and a written explanation of how it works. Their invention could be designed to accomplish a task such as tidying up their bedroom, feeding the dog, folding the laundry, playing a game of marbles, and so on.

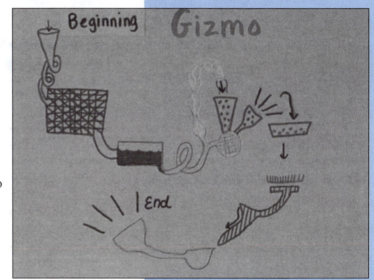

When the students finish their first draft/sketch of the diagram and written explanation, have them work with a partner to see what changes need to be made. Suggest that each partner try to follow the sequence of the workings of the invention, first by reading the diagram itself, and then by noting how it matches with the written explanation. The pairs can talk about changes that could be made to the diagram and explanation. The final diagram and written instructions could be placed in a classroom inventions folder.

 See **Assess Learning**, page 99.

The House That Jack Built

This is the house that Jack built.

This is the malt
That lay in the house
    that Jack built.

This is the rat,
That ate the malt
That lay in the house
    that Jack built.

This is the cat,
That killed the rat,
That ate the malt
That lay in the house
    that Jack built.

LINK TO CURRICULUM

Language Arts

Write a Sequence Poem

Read aloud the poem "The House that Jack Built" and ask students to listen to the rhythm and sequence pattern. Using the poem as a model, they can write a poem describing their own invention or the one of Paula's in the story.

Language Arts/The Arts

Perform a Readers' Theatre

Invite the students to work in small groups to perform "Anti-Snore Machine" as a readers' theatre presentation. Suggest that they first go through the story to note which parts will require a narrator, and which words won't be necessary to say (for example, the speakers tags). They might also want to consider using sound effects to add to the humor of the story. They could perform their readings for other classes in the school, particularly younger grades.

Health

Find Out About Snoring

Interested students can make a list of questions they'd like to find answers to about snoring. To find the answers to these questions, they can talk to people who know something about snoring and check books and the Internet. Their questions and answers can be written on paper strips and tacked up on the bulletin board for others to read.

- Why do people snore?
- Why do they stop when they're turned on their sides?
- What other things can be done to help people stop snoring?
- Why are there so many different sounds people make when they snore?
- Do people breathe properly when they snore?
- Is snoring dangerous to a person's health?

Science/Mathematics

Find Out About Noise Levels

Some students may be interested in investigating how noise level is measured, bylaws regulating acceptable noise levels where they live, what things make the loudest sounds, and so on. They might also like to search for interesting records about sounds, for example, what is the loudest snore ever measured. Their findings can be shared with the class.

Assess Learning

Visual Communication (see p. 97)

First, students can do a **self-assessment** of the diagram of their invention and their written explanation, using a checklist and rating scale similar to the ones below:

Check for these features
- drawings of objects
- labels for objects
- arrows showing the direction of flow of events and movement of objects
- beginning and end marked
- objects numbered in correct sequence
- name for invention
- small picture showing the end result

Rate these features (3—very good to 0—not at all)

Diagram Rating Scale				
1. Diagram matches the written description	3	2	1	0
2. Diagram/instructions clear/easily understood	3	2	1	0
3. Diagram neatly done	3	2	1	0

The same checklist and rating scale can be used by each partner in a **peer assessment** before the diagram and written description are put into the class folder.

Listen with Your Eyes

This article, by Sharon Stewart, tells of the varied ways messages are communicated through body language, and illustrates how these messages can vary with cultures, situations, and a person's own comfort zone.

Anthology, pages 64-68   **Blackline Masters 15 and 16**

Learning Choices

LINK TO EXPERIENCE

List Ways to Get Messages from People

Act Out a Title

READ AND RESPOND TO TEXT

READING FOCUS
- read a variety of fiction and non-fiction materials for different purposes
- STRATEGY: **read, paraphrase, and teach**

Assessment

REVIST THE TEXT

mini LESSONS

READING
Identify Ways of Providing Information
- identify different forms of writing and describe their characteristics

WRITING
Language Workshop — Style
- produce pieces of writing using a variety of forms, techniques, and resources appropriate to the form and purpose

Assessment

VISUAL COMMUNICATION
Perform a Mime
- use tone of voice and gestures to enhance the message and help convince or persuade listeners in conversations, discussions, or presentations

LINK TO CURRICULUM

LANGUAGE ARTS
Write a One-Act Pantomime

THE ARTS
Listen to a Conductor

SOCIAL STUDIES
Make a Cultural Gestures Book

MATHEMATICS
Create an Orbital Diagram

SCIENCE
Learn About the Body Language of an Animal

Key Learning Expectations

Students will
- read a variety of fiction and non-fiction materials for different purposes (**Reading Focus, p. 101**)
- identify different forms of writing and describe their characteristics (**Reading Mini Lesson, p. 102**)
- produce pieces of writing using a variety of forms, techniques, and resources appropriate to the form and purpose (**Writing Mini Lesson, p. 102**)
- use tone of voice and gestures to enhance the message and help convince or persuade listeners in conversations, discussions, or presentations (**Visual Communication Mini Lesson, p. 104**)

LINK TO EXPERIENCE

List Ways to Get Messages from People

Have the students brainstorm various ways they get messages from people—phone calls, fax and e-mail, letters, cards, conversations, gestures and hand signals, facial expression, body movements and gestures, messages on bulletin boards or fridges, and so on. List their suggestions on the board and ask the students to categorize them; for example, written, verbal, non-verbal, ...

Act Out a Title

In small groups, the students can play "Charades." Individuals use their bodies and gestures to act out the name of a song, book, or television show, while the others in the group try to "read" the actions and guess the title.

READ AND RESPOND TO TEXT

Reading Focus

Students can use a **read, paraphrase, and teach** strategy to read assigned sections of the article, summarize the information, and teach it to others in their group.

The jigsaw co-operative learning technique can be used to organize the reading and sharing of information. Arrange the students in home groups of four, giving each member a number to match the four sections of the article. In their study groups, suggest that the students try the activity if there is one in their section, as well as reading and discussing the text.

When the students go back into their home groups, have them share what they learned from their section.

GENERAL JIGSAW STRATEGY

Students are put into "home" or original groups, where each group member is given a number. The home groups separate, and each member joins a new group, formed by students with the same number from the home groups. These new "expert" groups are the study groups where the students become experts at an assigned task.

When the task is complete, members of the expert groups return to their home groups. The students teach the other home group members what they learned in their expert groups. In this way, all the students become familiar with all the information.

Reader Response

Students could
- hold a conversation about the article to discuss questions such as:
  - **What is the difference between "intentional" and "unintentional" body language?**
  - **What gestures or facial expressions do you use quite often?**
  - **What do you do when you feel embarrassed or uncomfortable?**
  - **Have you ever been in a situation where you misunderstood a person's gestures or facial expressions? What happened?**
  - **What problems do you think could arise from masking one's feelings?**
  - **What value is there in "listening with your eyes"?**
- use the text and their own interpretations to write definitions for gaze behavior, regulators, personal space zones, eyebrows flash, cue.
- choose a sport and make a chart showing the signals used by participants and referees, umpires, judges, ...
- keep a notebook record of body language observed over a certain period.
- create a mini catalogue of symbolic gestures.

Introduce the article to students by reading the introduction aloud, then discussing how the introduction helps them understand what is meant by the title, "Listen with Your Eyes."

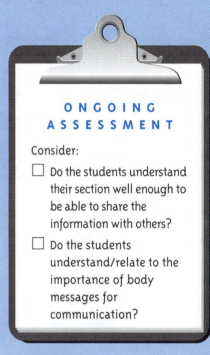

ONGOING ASSESSMENT

Consider:
- ☐ Do the students understand their section well enough to be able to share the information with others?
- ☐ Do the students understand/relate to the importance of body messages for communication?

REVISIT THE TEXT

Reading

Identify Ways of Providing Information

Have the students revisit the text to find structural features of the article that helped them to understand and visualize the information presented. Elicit the use of:
- definitions given in the text
- important terms written in italics
- examples used throughout
- "Try This" suggestions in sidebars
- section headings

Talk with the students about the value of each of these features, for example:
- if definitions are given in text, then the reader doesn't have to stop to figure out the word or look it up in a dictionary
- text in sidebar separates information that is interesting or helpful, but not really part of the main text, from the main part. This way you don't get confused by the extra information.

Begin a chart listing helpful features and encourage the students to use it as a reminder of things that can help in reading comprehension and in making their own writing clearer.

Provide an opportunity for the students to look through reference materials to find other examples of features like these and add them to the chart.

Writing

Language Workshop — Style

Blackline Master 15

Working with italics first, have the students skim throught the selection to locate words written in italics and determine how and why italics are used in each case. Then suggest that they look back through anthology selections they have already read, and look for different uses of italics. As they discover the different uses of italics, jot down explanations and examples on a chart.

In material that is handwritten, each word or letter that would be in italics is underlined.

Helpful Features

- definitions in text
- sidebars
- photos and diagrams
- eye-catching graphics
-

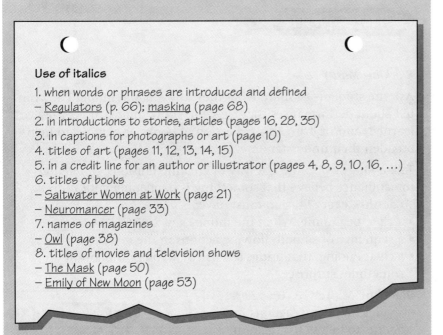

Use of italics

1. when words or phrases are introduced and defined
– <u>Regulators</u> (p. 66); <u>masking</u> (page 68)
2. in introductions to stories, articles (pages 16, 28, 35)
3. in captions for photographs or art (page 10)
4. titles of art (pages 11, 12, 13, 14, 15)
5. in a credit line for an author or illustrator (pages 4, 8, 9, 10, 16, …)
6. titles of books
– <u>Saltwater Women at Work</u> (page 21)
– <u>Neuromancer</u> (page 33)
7. names of magazines
– <u>Owl</u> (page 38)
8. titles of movies and television shows
– <u>The Mask</u> (page 50)
– <u>Emily of New Moon</u> (page 53)

Encourage the students to look through other printed materials for more and different examples of how italics are used. For example:
9. words that are from another language
– See if you can find what the Spanish word *noche* means
10. scientific terms
– The species name of the monarch butterfly is *danaus plexippus*

Next, work with quotation marks. Begin by explaining that, for some of the uses in the "Uses of Italics" list above, quotation marks may be used instead of italics; that it is a matter of choice. Have the students skim through "Listen with Your Eyes" to find an example of this. Then ask them to find two other uses of quotation marks in the selection and discuss these.

Make a chart, with examples, to review these uses of quotation marks.

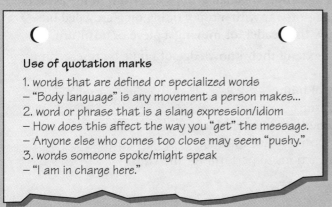

Use of quotation marks

1. words that are defined or specialized words
– "Body language" is any movement a person makes...
2. word or phrase that is a slang expression/idiom
– How does this affect the way you "get" the message.
– Anyone else who comes too close may seem "pushy."
3. words someone spoke/might speak
– "I am in charge here."

Students can complete Blackline Master 15, *Uses of Italics and Quotation Marks,* for practice in applying what they have learned.

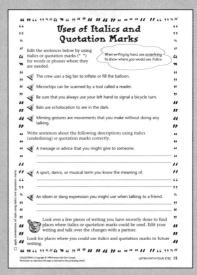

Blackline Master 15

 Assessment See **Assess Learning**, page 106.

BOOKS ON MIME

Exploring Mime. Mark Stolzenberg. Sterling, 1979.

Mime: Basics for Beginners. Cindie and Matthew Straub. Plays, 1984.

Mime: The Steps Beyond Words: for the Actors of Dance and Drama. Adrian Peknold. N. C. Press, 1982.

All About Mime: Understanding and Performing the Expressive Silence. Maravene Sheppard Loeschke. Prentice-Hall, 1982.

Mime and Masks. Roberta Nobleman. New Plays Books, 1979.

Visual Communication

Perform a Mime

Blackline Master 16

Ask the students to share what they know about mime. They can tell about performances they've seen, show some actions they've learned, and/or bring in a collection of books or pictures to help broaden their understanding.

Talk about how mime is a way of creating illusions; of making the audience believe that something is happening with nothing. To do this, every illusion must have:
• a clear beginning, when the mime "gets set"
• a sequence of smooth flowing actions in the middle
• a clear ending, that brings a sense of accomplishment or sometimes surprise

Blackline Master 16, *Up a Rope,* provides mime instructions for students to follow to create the illusion of climbing a rope. Make an overhead transparency or provide pairs of students with copies. They can take turns following the directions to mime the action and critiquing each other's performances.

After reading and following these, individual students can mime other illusion movements like going down the rope, unwrapping a gift, looking in the mirror, waiting for and riding in an elevator, blowing up a balloon, or walking a tightrope. In small groups, they can mime actions like playing tug-of-war with a rope, riding on a crowded bus, playing Follow the Leader, or moving a piece of furniture.

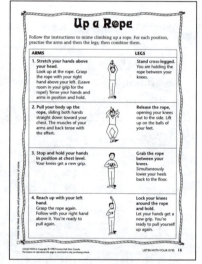

Blackline Master 16

Students can extend their knowledge of mime by researching such aspects as
• the history of mime
• mime make-up
• famous mimes like Marcel Marceau
• basic body positions for miming
• more mime actions to perform for the class

LINK TO CURRICULUM

Language Arts

Write a One-Act Pantomime

Interested students could write a short, one-act play that involves no speaking. Their script could consist of a summary of the plot, broken down into action segments, and suggestions for each of the character's gestures, facial expressions, actions, and use of props in the segments. They could then work with a small group to put on the pantomime for others, using make-up and costumes if they wish.

The Arts

Listen to a Conductor

Make arrangements for a choir or orchestra director to come into the classroom to talk with students about the importance of conducting and to demonstrate some of the directing signals used. Or, you could show the students a video about choir or orchestra conducting. Following the visit or video, interested students could make a chart showing various signals used by conductors.

Social Studies

Make a Cultural Gestures Book

Invite the students to use a variety of resources such as books, the Internet, film documentaries, other students, and people they know to find out about gestures used in different cultures. They can write up and perhaps illustrate these gestures in a "Did You Know" booklet.

For purposes here, **pantomime** is considered to be the telling of a story through the use of body movements only. Students might be interested in knowing that a pantomime was originally a farcical, romantic comedy based on a fairy tale that was performed during the Christmas season.

Mathematics

Create an Orbital Diagram

Following the pattern of the Personal Space Zones on page 67, students can make an orbital diagram comparing distances for five students: how far they live from school, or the metres each one can throw a ball, or the metres each one can run in a minute, ...

Or, some students could do a personal study of their own comfort zones with different people and diagram this in their own personal space zone diagram.

Science

Learn About the Body Language of an Animal

Talk with the students about how animals use body language as a way of communication and invite them to share what they know. Interested students can research a particular animal to find out how it uses its body to communicate. They can record the information they find on a class wall chart.

> **Animal Body Language**
>
> Wolf
> The wolf's tail
> - held high shows that it is the *dominant* wolf
> - hanging low *means* the wolf is relaxed
> - slightly curved upwards might mean it's going to attack
> - tucked between its legs shows that the wolf has submitted

 Students could search the Internet or *Encarta* to learn more about the body language of animals. See pages 5 and (ii) for resource information.

 Assessment

Assess Learning

Writing (see p. 102)

Focus on a few students during the lesson for **teacher assessment.** Make notes on each student for questions such as:
- Does the student participate in looking for examples in the text?
- Can the student identify uses of italics and quotation marks?
- Do his/her responses indicate an understanding of the use of these features?

Use Blackline Master 15 as a **work sample** for all students. You might wish to hold a conference with the students observed during the lesson to discuss their blackline master to gain further knowledge of their understanding of the use of italics and quotation marks.

Dancing the Cotton-Eyed Joe

In this short story by Joann Mazzio, a young boy befriends a blind girl and learns that having a physical disability doesn't have to hamper one's life.

Anthology, pages 69-73   Blackline Masters 17 and 26
Learning Strategy Card 50

Learning Choices

LINK TO EXPERIENCE

Talk About Dances and Dancing

Write About Making a Friend

READ AND RESPOND TO TEXT

READING FOCUS
* make predictions while reading a story or novel, using various clues
* STRATEGY: **narrated reading**

REVISIT THE TEXT

mini LESSONS

READING
Reading Between the Lines
* explain their interpretation of a written work, supporting it with evidence from the work and from their own knowledge and experience

WRITING
Write and Revise a Personal Narrative
* use a variety of sentence types and sentence structures appropriate for their purposes
Language Workshop — Spelling
* word pairs; 3-syllable words

ORAL COMMUNICATION
Follow a Square Dance Call
* follow detailed instructions

LINK TO CURRICULUM

LANGUAGE ARTS
Read Stories About People with Disabilities

SCIENCE/HEALTH
Research Blindness

MATHEMATICS
Design a Budget

THE ARTS
Learn a Dance

Key Learning Expectations

Students will
* make predictions while reading a story or novel, using various clues (**Reading Focus, p. 108**)
* explain their interpretation of a written work, supporting it with evidence from the work and from their own knowledge and experience (**Reading Mini Lesson, p. 109**)
* use a variety of sentence types and sentence structures appropriate for their purposes (**Writing Mini Lesson, p. 110**)
* follow detailed instructions (**Oral Communication Mini Lesson, p. 112**)

LINK TO EXPERIENCE

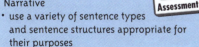

Talk About Dances and Dancing

Ask the students to recall an experience where they have attended a dance (school dance, wedding dance) and/or the dances they are able to do. In small groups, have them discuss dancing, perhaps using questions like the following to guide the discussion.
* Which dance do you find easy to do? Why?
* Which dance is difficult? Why?
* Who has taught you some dances? Have you taught others a dance? What was the experience like?
* What do you like/dislike about dancing?

Write About Making a Friend

Ask the students to think about a friend they have and how they met that friend. Have them write about the event in their journals, telling how they felt about the person at the time, if they knew they were going to be friends right then, what was easy or difficult about the meeting, ...,. Encourage them to share their entries with a classmate if they wish.

Reading Focus

Use a **narrated reading** strategy. As you read the first section aloud, suggest that the students close their eyes and picture themselves as the young person arriving at a dance on a wintery night. At the end of the section, invite the students to predict what might happen next and why they think so. The students then read the next section to confirm their predictions. Continue reading the story in this way, alternating turns. Following are suggested story divisions and prompts for predicting.

Suggested Story Divisions

Teacher read aloud: To the end of "'Have a good time tonight, honey,' said Mrs. Taylor." (page 70)
Stop, discuss, and predict what kind of a dance this is and what things you would expect to see at a dance like this.

Student passage: To the end of "… and fathers teach the daughters." (page 70)
Discuss and check predictions.

Teacher read aloud: To the end of "… then touched the top of my head." (page 71)
Stop, discuss, and predict who this girl might be, why she is dressed differently from the others, and why she is acting in a strange manner.

Student passage: To the end of "… as if she were daring me." (page 72)
Discuss and check predictions.

Teacher read aloud: To the end of " … where she had been sitting."(page 73)
Stop, discuss, and predict what Mark and Alice will do next.

Student passage: To the end of "… learned anything so fast in my life." (page 73)
Discuss and check predictions.

Teacher read aloud: To the end of the story.

Following the reading, discuss the story as a whole group, talking about what surprised the students in the story, how they felt about the blind girl, and what they think the young boy learned from attending this dance.

Reader Response

Students could
• illustrate a favorite scene from the story.
• discuss words, events, or the kind of dances in the story that may be new to them.

- write in their journals about the ways that this story is like other stories they have read or viewed.
- work in small groups to role-play a scene from the story.
- think of questions they could ask Alice about her blindness, such as what are the most difficult things for her to do, does she have a seeing eye dog, ...

REVISIT THE TEXT

Reading

Reading Between the Lines

Blackline Master 17

Explain to the students that authors carefully choose which details they will include in their stories. These details give direct information about the characters, setting, or plot. The reader can also draw conclusions about the story based on the details, even though this information is not directly stated. This is called "reading between the lines," and the conclusions a reader makes are called "inferences."

Ask the students to reread the first page of the story to find the main story details. Jot these on the board. Then ask them to read between the lines to make inferences that are supported by or make sense according to the story details. Have them give their reasons for their inferences as well. For example:

Story Details	Inferences/Reasons
– country-western dances are held at Lake Valley on Saturday night – Lake Valley is a ghost town – Mark had been going since he was a baby – he's eleven years old now – he's learned the polka, waltz, and schottische	– They hold the dances at Lake Valley because it doesn't cost anything to use the schoolhouse, or because no one will complain about the noise. – Mark probably learned to dance at Lake Valley dances since he's been going there for such a long time.

Discuss with the students how reading between the lines makes the story richer and more interesting and helps them become more involved in the story.

Students can complete Blackline Master 17, *Reading Between the Lines*, with a partner. Suggest that they share and compare their notes with another pair.

In reading between the lines, the reader should think about what things they find out about the characters, the plot, and the setting without being told directly.

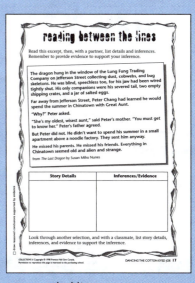

Blackline Master 17

You might wish to work through the blackline master with any students who appear to have difficulty with the concept of inferring.

Write and Revise a Personal Narrative

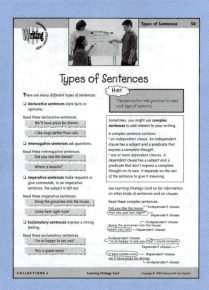

Learning Strategy Card 50

Discuss with the students why "Dancing the Cotton-Eyed Joe" is a good example of a personal narrative. Jot their ideas on the board or chart. For example:

• the story was told from the "I" point of view and told how the main character felt
• it has a beginning and ending
• story told where the events took place.
• the events were told in the order they happened.
• the story told who the characters in the story were
• it used descriptive language

Ask the students to think about a personal experience they would like to write about, then have them begin work on their first draft of the narrative. Upon completion of their draft, suggest that they first look through it on their own or with a partner to check if they have followed the points they discussed about what makes a good narrative.

Once the students are satisfied with the content of their narrative, talk about the structure of their sentences by suggesting that the inclusion of complex sentences could enhance their narrative and make it more interesting to read.

Write the following example on the board:

• Although some dogs can perform tricks, most of them cannot.
• As you can see, the dog trainers can be very creative.
• Because so many people attended the parade, they had to add five more benches for seating.

Discuss the structure of these complex sentences, eliciting that they are made of one independent clause and one dependent clause.

Learning Strategy Card 50, *Types of Sentences*, provides more explanations and examples of complex sentences and dependent and independent clauses. You may want to refer to it during your discussion with the students, and/or suggest that individual students make use of the information and practice activities provided on the card.

Have the students revisit the selection to find two or three examples of complex sentences to share with a partner.

Ask the students to take a second look through their personal narrative and locate complex sentences they may have already written. As well, suggest that they look for places where they could revise their writing to include complex sentences to enhance the piece.

 See **Assess Learning**, page 114.

A clause in a sentence that can stand alone is called an **independent clause**. A clause that can't stand alone is called a **dependent clause**. A **complex sentence** is made up of one independent clause and one or more dependent clauses.

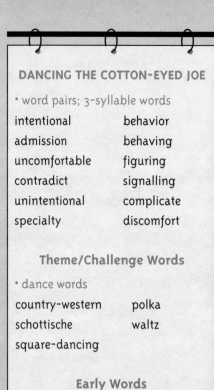

Blackline Master 26

Explore and Discover

Use Blackline Master 26 and the **sort, share, discuss,** and **chart** procedure outlined on page 17 to work with the words.

In discussing the words, work with students to determine the root word for the word pairs and then make word webs for each pair. One web can be made as a group and the others by students on their own. Clap out the syllables in the other list words and note which ones have affixes that add syllables to them.

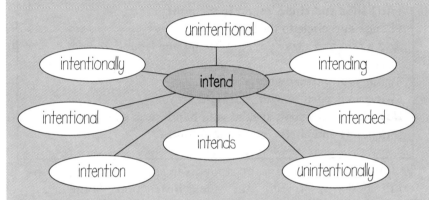

Follow this exploration with a **pretest, study and practise,** and a **post test** as outlined on page 17.

Study and Practise

Students could
- use Learning Strategy Card 4 to study words identified after the pretest.
- on the front of their word cards, write the number of syllables in the words and also highlight any letters in the word that could cause difficulty. They say the word softly in syllables, write it down as they do, and then check their spelling.
- play a memory game with a partner. The two partners select 10 matching word cards (two cards each of 10 different words) and put their cards face down in random order in 5 rows of 4. Alternately, students turn over one card and then another, trying to choose a card that is the same word as the one just turned over. If the word cards match and the student can spell the word correctly, he/she keeps the cards and turns over another two cards. If not, the two cards are turned face down again, and the other student takes a turn.

DANCING THE COTTON-EYED JOE

• word pairs; 3-syllable words

intentional	behavior
admission	behaving
uncomfortable	figuring
contradict	signalling
unintentional	complicate
specialty	discomfort

Theme/Challenge Words

• dance words

country-western	polka
schottische	waltz
square-dancing	

Early Words

• /oŭ/ sound

touches	young
couples	youngest
country	

Oral Communication

Follow a Square Dance Call

Discuss with the students what a square dance is, asking them to share any knowledge or personal experience they have. You might also want to play some square dances, with callers, for them to listen to.

Then arrange the students in partners to try some square dance steps. Give the following set of oral instructions for the pairs to follow. Encourage them to listen carefully to the instructions before they try them. Repeat the call until all the pairs can follow the instructions.

> Join hands and circle 'round to the right,
> Change and circle to the left,
> Add a skip and shake your hip 'round and 'round you go.
>
> Swing your partner with your left,
> Swing your partner with your right,
> Now skip on the spot, shakin' your hands with all your might
> Join hands and circle 'round and 'round.

Following the dance, ask the students to share their suggestions on the best ways to follow the caller's instructions. Some ideas could be:
– visualize the steps before you dance
– listen carefully to the caller
– go slow at first and when comfortable, you can speed up
– partners should practise over and over

To extend the activity, small groups of students could work together to compose instructions for a square dance for partners or for squares of partners of two pairs or more. One of the students in the group could take the role of the caller, while other students in the group perform the dance. After practising, the groups could show their dances to one another.

LINK TO CURRICULUM

Language Arts

Read Stories About People with Disabilities

Invite the students to read books about people with disabilities. They could then get together in discussion groups to talk about how the people in their books learned to cope with their disability, how others reacted to their disability, what they personally learned

You might want to enlist the help of the physical education teacher or someone from the community who has experience with calling to lead the students through some square dance steps.

STORIES ABOUT SPECIAL PEOPLE

Eddie's Blue-Winged Dragon. Carole Adler. G. P. Putnam, 1988.

What Difference Does It Make, Danny? Helen Young. A. Deutsch, 1980.

Who Will Take Care of Me? Patricia Hermes. Harcourt Brace Jovanovich, 1983.

Edith, Herself. Ellen Howard. Atheneum, 1987.

Circle of Giving. Ellen Howard. Macmillan, 1984.

from the book, and so on. Encourage the students to share any personal experience that the stories call to mind.

Students could read the selection entitled , "Little by Little" by Jean Little, which is found in the grade four unit, *And the Message Is...* , and talk about the selection in discussion groups.

Science/Health

Research Blindness

In groups, invite the students to brainstorm a list of questions they have about blindness; for example, what are some of the causes of blindness, are there degrees of blindness, what kind of help is available to the blind, ... Suggest that they use a number of sources to find answers to their questions: books, the Internet, the CNIB, blind people, ...

Each group could write a one-page fact sheet of important points of information it found about the topic.

Mathematics

Design a Budget

Pairs of students could imagine that they have been hired to plan and organize an event (school dance, patrol party, a barbeque, team dinner, ...) and that they will be responsible for the budget. This will include setting the prices for the tickets, pricing out the food, the entertainment, the accommodations, and so on.

They can prepare a budget sheet that sets out all the expenses they will need to pay out and all the sources of revenue they can expect/will need to get. Invite pairs of students to share and compare their budget designs with one another to see if there is anything else they may need to include.

To extend the activity, the students could conduct research to put actual numbers into the budget and work towards developing a completed budget.

The Arts

Some students might want to learn one of the dances from the selection or another one of their choosing, such as traditional dances from various cultures. Suggest that they find someone who is willing to come to the class to teach the dance. Or, there may be a student in the school who would be willing to teach a dance. Or, some group members could learn the dance from a family member and teach it to others.

The homework project for Week 4 is to learn a dance from a family member. See *Home Connections Newsletter*, Blackline Master 2.

A s s e s s   L e a r n i n g

Writing (see p. 110)

Select teams of two or three students to **peer assess** the personal narratives. Make sure that each student has the opportunity to complete an assessment. Discuss, collaborate on, and post the criteria for assessment in advance.

The peer group assessors could share their feedback with the writer, explaining their ratings. Then the assessments could be attached to the narratives and stored as **work samples** in the students' portfolios.

The students could use a personal narrative rating scale similar to the one shown, where 1 is the lowest and 3 the highest. Or, they may wish to use a "word" scale, such as "most of the time," "some of the time," or "not at all."

Personal Narrative Rating Scale			
1. told where events took place	1	2	3
2. events written in order they happened with a beginning and ending	1	2	3
3. named/described people who were involved	1	2	3
4. used clear and descriptive language	1	2	3
5. "I" voice of writer used; strong evidence of character's feelings	1	2	3

AND/OR

Use the narratives as a **performance assessment** of the students' ability to write complex sentences and to make the necessary revisions to their narrative to include them.
Look at drafts of the narrative to assess whether students have
• written correct complex sentences.
• made revisions to their narrative to include complex sentences.

Record your assessment as an **anecdotal comment** in your record book. Students could date their stories and place them in their portfolios as a work sample for the unit.

All the Places to Love

In this picture book story, Patricia MacLachlan tells of a family's special places and why they hold importance for them. In doing so, she reminds us of our special places.

Anthology, pages 74-77
Blackline Master 18

Patricia MacLachlan is also the author of *Journey,* one of the novels for this unit.

Learning Choices

LINK TO EXPERIENCE

Draw a Special Place

List and Categorize Places

READ AND RESPOND TO TEXT

READING FOCUS
• explain their interpretation of a written work, supporting it with evidence from the work and from their own knowledge and experience
• STRATEGY: **listen and read along**

REVISIT THE TEXT

mini LESSONS

READING
Identify Story Themes

Assessment

• summarize and explain the main ideas in information materials, and cite details that support the main ideas

WRITING
Write a Memory Poem

Assessment

• communicate ideas and information for a variety of purposes and to specific audiences

VISUAL COMMUNICATION
Compare Illustration and Text

Assessment

• analyze and assess a media work and express a considered viewpoint about it

LINK TO CURRICULUM

LANGUAGE ARTS
Find Similes

Play "Categories"

LANGUAGE ARTS/THE ARTS
Illustrate a Cluster of Words

Design a Birth Announcement Card

SCIENCE
Draw and Label Plants and Animals

Key Learning Expectations

Students will
• explain their interpretation of a written work, supporting it with evidence from the work and from their own knowledge and experience (**Reading Focus, p. 116**)
• summarize and explain the main ideas in information materials, and cite details that support the main ideas (**Reading Mini Lesson, p. 116**)
• communicate ideas and information for a variety of purposes and to specific audiences (**Writing Mini Lesson, p. 117**)
• analyze and assess a media work and express a considered viewpoint about it (**Visual Communication Mini Lesson, p. 118**)

LINK TO EXPERIENCE

Draw a Special Place

Invite the students to draw a picture about a place that is very special to them. Ask them to write a description for their picture, telling why it is special to them; for example, the place may be where they share good times with friends or family, where they go when they want to be alone, and so on.

In small groups, the students can share their picture and description with each other.

List and Categorize Places

Read the title of the selection, "All the Places to Love," to the students and ask them to brainstorm the names of places that could be part of such a list. The names of places can be ones they know from personal experience, from others' experiences, from books, or from their own imaginations.

Working together in groups of four or five, students can categorize the items in the list, for example, unusual places, common places, exciting places, quiet places, ..., . They might want to add other places to the categories as they work.

Reading Focus

Use a variation of the **listen and read along** strategy. Read the selection aloud as the students listen. Encourage them to let their minds roam free and just enjoy the selection. Invite them to share their impressions of the story and how it made them feel. Then read the selection a second time as the students follow along. Ask them to look for descriptive language that they particularly like.

Arrange the students in small groups to share the descriptions they enjoyed and talk about the images they saw in their minds as they read those parts.

Reader Response

Students could

• read the selection to a classmate using intonation, inflection, and expression to give their own interpretation of the text.
• write about an event in their own lives that involves a special place.
• describe one of the characters from the story.
• make a timeline outlining the events of the story.
•  survey family members about their special places.

REVISIT THE TEXT

mini LESSON

Reading

Identify Story Themes

Have students reread the selection, then discuss what they think is the main or most important theme of the story. Ask them to find supporting evidence from the selection for their theme, using words and phrases from the selection and their own interpretation of what the author meant. Organize their responses in a web or diagram.

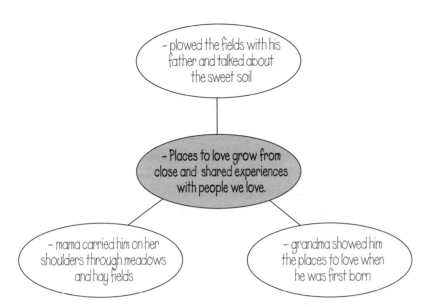

Then talk about how stories often have other minor themes; that is, the author may have more than one message or idea he or she wants to express. Ask the students to brainstorm other themes, for example:

– the connection among generations of family is important
– life is like a big circle
– we learn things from our family
– places in nature can be magical/special

Arrange the students in groups to choose one of the brainstormed themes or choose one of their own and make a web or diagram showing details that support the theme. Bring the groups together to share their webs or diagrams.

Discuss this pattern for organizing their ideas, where a theme or main idea is supported by a number of details, and how organizing this information can help them understand what they are reading.

Writing

Write a Memory Poem

Blackline Master 18

Provide the students with copies of Blackline Master 18, *Memory Poems*, or make an overhead transparency. Read the poems and the authors' comments about writing the poems. Ask the students what the poets did either to get ready to begin their poem or to write it. Discuss the comments and talk about other things writers can do to help them write a poem about a memory. Make a list of all the suggestions.

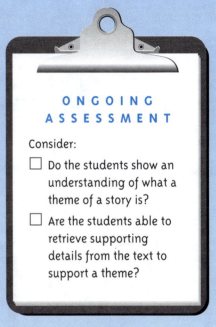

Blackline Master 18

To write a memory poem

- choose a topic/memory that is a close experience
- close your eyes and revisit the memory, recalling your feelings, the sounds, the colors, your reactions,...
- on a think sheet, write down all the important words and phrases that came to mind as you were visualizing
- write similes, metaphors, and other figurative language that come from your ideas on the think sheet

Ask the students to recall memorable events that have occurred in their lives and to compose a poem about one of their memories, using suggestions from the list and any type of poem they wish.

Have students come together in small groups to share their memory poem and talk about how/if the suggestions were of assistance to them as they composed their poems.

 Using a word processing program such as *Creative Writer 2*, students could recopy their poem and add appropriate background colors that they think best suit their poem. (See pages 5 and (ii) for resource information.)

Assessment See **Assess Learning**, page 120.

Visual Communication

Compare Illustration and Text

Read page 76 of "All the Places to Love" aloud as the students view the illustration that accompanies the text. Talk about the illustration and the text, using questions such as:
- Does the illustration show a person, place, or event described in the text?
- How well does the illustration match the description of the place Mama loves best?
- What does the illustration add to the text? What does the text add to the illustration?
- What techniques did the illustrator use to make the illustration look so real?
- If you were the artist, what would you do differently?

Have the students choose another illustration from this story or from another story they have read and examine how the illustration works together to enhance the descriptions and feelings conveyed in the selection. Encourage them to think about the questions used in the group discussion to guide their thinking. Then arrange them in small groups to talk about their illustration and explain their impressions of the relationship between the text and the illustration.

LINK TO CURRICULUM

Language Arts

Find Similes

Write on the board the simile, "Crows in the dirt that swaggered like pirates," taken from the selection. With the students, revisit the purpose and structure of similes in stories and in poems. Invite them to return to the selection and find examples of how the author used similes to create vivid imagery for readers.

The students could write the examples they find on a classroom chart and add other similes they like from other readings. The chart could be posted in the Writing Centre for students to use as a reference for future writing projects.

Play "Categories"

Write the following list of topics from the selection on the board. To play a category game, one student acts as the gamekeeper and chooses a topic. The students work independently or in pairs to brainstorm as many items as they can that fit within the category in a certain time limit. Students then share their lists and get one point for each correct item in a category. The person/team with the most points after all the categories are called is the winner. The students may wish to extend this game by developing categories of their own.

- something made of wool
- animals found in woods/forests
- water games
- things you need to take care of a baby
- things you need to take care of farm animals

Language Arts/The Arts

Illustrate a Cluster of Words

Students could choose five or six words from the selection that are related in some way and write them on a large sheet of paper in whatever design they wish. To accompany the words, have them draw or paint images and/or designs that compliment the words and help the viewer understand their meanings.

Design a Birth Announcement Card

Have the students suggest various reasons for sending a birth announcement. Show a variety of cards and talk about how the cards' designs and messages complement one another. Students could then design a card announcing the birth of someone recently born in their family, or they may wish to design a card telling of their birth. Invite the students to share their cards with one another.

Science

Draw and Label Plants and Animals

Invite the students to revisit the selection and jot down the names of plants and animals the author referred to in her story; for example: cattails, killdeers, marsh marigolds, marsh hawks, turtle, wild turkeys, ...

Students could choose two or three from the list and locate appropriate information about the animals and/or plants. They could also draw diagrams/illustrations and label them. The information could be displayed or made into a class booklet.

Assess Learning

Writing (see p. 117)

Hold **group conferences** with three students at a time to assess the process of writing they undertook to complete their poem. Ask the students to point out the steps they took to prepare and compose their poem. Assess whether the students
• used preplanning strategies such as brainstorming, visualizing, and/or organizing a think sheet
• used ideas from the think sheet to create similes and metaphors
• produced a poem related to the topic of memories

Use the opportunity to praise students for the steps they used to write their poem, and by questioning, help them see where they might have been able to use additional steps.

Speak Your Dreams

These poems, "The Dream Keeper" and "To You" by Langston Hughes, express the power and need to hold on to our dreams in the hopes that they may be realized.

Anthology, pages 78-79
Blackline Masters 19, 20, and 21

Learning Choices

LINK TO EXPERIENCE

Talk About Personal Dreams

Brainstorm Descriptive Words

READ AND RESPOND TO TEXT

READING FOCUS
• understand the vocabulary and language structures appropriate for this grade level
• STRATEGY: listen and sketch

REVISIT THE TEXT

READING
Personalize a Reader Response
• explain their interpretation of a written work, supporting it with evidence from the work and from their own knowledge and experience

WRITING
Discuss Hyphenated Words
• use correctly the conventions of spelling

ORAL COMMUNICATION
Memorize a Poem for Presentation
• use tone of voice and gestures to enhance the message and help convince or persuade listeners in conversations, discussions, or presentations

LINK TO CURRICULUM

LANGUAGE ARTS
Audio-Tape a Poem

SOCIAL STUDIES
Discuss Solutions for Problems

SCIENCE
Find Out About Dreams and Dreaming

THE ARTS
Make a Dream Catcher

Key Learning Expectations

Students will
• understand the vocabulary and language structures appropriate for this grade level (Reading Focus, p. 122)
• explain their interpretation of a written work, supporting it with evidence from the work and from their own knowledge and experience (Reading Mini Lesson, p. 122)
• use correctly the conventions of spelling (Writing Mini Lesson, p. 123)
• use tone of voice and gestures to enhance the message and help convince or persuade listeners in conversations, discussions, or presentations (Oral Communication Mini Lesson, p. 124)

LINK TO EXPERIENCE

Talk About Personal Dreams

Arrange the students in pairs or small groups to talk about their personal dreams. They can use questions like the following to guide their discussion.
• What are some of the dreams you have for yourself and for others?
• Which of your dreams have come to be?
• Is it wrong to dream things that could not possibly happen? Why?
• If you were to tell someone what it means to have a dream, how would you describe it?

Brainstorm Descriptive Words

As a group, brainstorm words and phrases that could be used to describe dreams and dreaming. Once the list has been generated, discuss the connection of each word to dreams.

— a sense of hope
— forward thinking
— personal
— feeling free
— whole

— daydreams, night dreams
— desires
— floating
— connected

Get Ready to Read

Read the titles of the two poems to the students. Discuss
— what the titles make them think about
— what they think the poems will be about

Reading Focus

Use a variation of the listen and visualize strategy, **listen and sketch**. Read the poems aloud to the students and ask them to picture in their minds images suggested by the poems. Then provide each student with a large piece of paper. Read the poems aloud a second time and ask them to quickly sketch the images. Encourage them to draw as many images as they visualize.

Following the readings, the students might like to reread the poems on their own and refine their sketches, perhaps adding color. Then have the students share their art work and explain their images, perhaps in small groups.

The pictures could be displayed under the title "Images and Dreams."

Reader Response

Students could
• discuss figures of speech in the poems with a partner, talking about their meanings and what they add to the poems.
• read the poems to a partner.
• write in their journal about their own personal dreams and aspirations.
• find and read other poems and books about the topic of dreams.
• illustrate a title page for one of the two poems.

REVISIT THE TEXT

Reading

Personalize a Reader Response

Blackline Master 19

Ask the students to reflect on some of the things they think about when they read or listen to a story or article; that is, how do they respond. List and discuss their ideas; for example:
• I think about the sad/happy things that happened.
• I remember similar things that have happened to me.
• I look for all the action. I love action stories and I like to compare them to action movies.

- If there are characters like me and my friends, then I remember the story.
- I have to like the story to respond. If I don't like it, I don't think much about it.

With the students, compile a list of things they could do to help guide their responses to their reading. The list could concentrate on the following three response ideas.

To make a good response:
- Think about your feelings—how the writing makes you feel or how you feel about the characters, plot, or setting; for example: " I like the way the girl in the story figures out things. She's neat."

- Make comparisons between something in the story and something in your own life or something you have read; for example: " The way the man treats his dog is so mean. He reminds me of our neighbor and how he yells at dogs who walk on his lawn. It's not their fault."

- Give an opinion about the writing or about an idea in the writing; for example: " This story does a good job of describing the scenes. You feel like you are there with the boys. When they are yelling, I think I can hear them."

To provide the students with further understanding as to how they can personalize their reading responses, have them complete Blackline Master 19, *Personal Reading Responses*. Discuss their responses as a class after they have completed the first section. Then have them complete the second section and share their responses with a partner.

To extend the activity, Invite the students to choose and read another selection from the anthology or another story, poem, or picture book they have read and respond to the reading by thinking of a comment for each of the three response ideas. Have them write their responses in their journals. They may wish to share their written responses with a classmate.

Writing

Discuss Hyphenated Words

Ask students to revisit the poem, "The Dream Keeper," and locate the hyphenated words. Write the words on the board. Discuss and list familiar hyphenated words. You might also want to have them look through other selections in the unit for examples.

Hyphenated Words
- cloud-cloth
- too-rough
- all-star
- sister-in-law
- twenty-three
- non-fiction

Reading is like being part of a discussion. Students should be encouraged to think about personal experiences connected to and their feelings about the story or article, or share them with someone, to help them understand better what they read.

Blackline Master 19

Reinforce with the students that the best place to check for hyphenation is in a dictionary. You might also want to talk about forming plurals of some hyphenated words, such as "sisters-in-law."

Ask the students if they know of any rules that would help them with hyphenation. Discuss what they know, and using this information and the examples generated, make a chart for reference.

HYPHENS

1. A hyphen is used in some compound nouns and with certain prefixes.
   Examples: gate-crasher, sister-in-law, ex-mayor, self-confident

2. A hyphen connects compound adjectives that come before nouns.
   Examples: high-speed train, part-time employee, long-term contract

3. Hyphens are used to spell out numbers from twenty-one through ninety-nine and fractions.
   Examples: forty-two, seventy-one, two-thirds

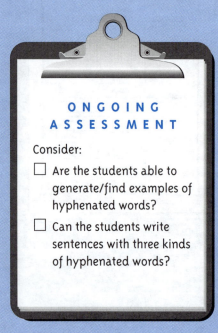

ONGOING ASSESSMENT

Consider:

☐ Are the students able to generate/find examples of hyphenated words?

☐ Can the students write sentences with three kinds of hyphenated words?

Ask pairs of students to compose four or five sentences that contain examples of these three types of hyphens. Arrange them in small groups to share and discuss their sentences.

To extend the activity, the students could go on a hyphenated word hunt to locate hyphenated words in their reading. The words could be listed in a wall chart, perhaps according to their beginning letters. This list could be referred to by students when involved with a writing activity.

Oral Communication

Memorize a Poem for Presentation

mini LESSON

Write the following portion of a poem on the board and ask the students to read it and suggest what they would need to do if they were going to memorize it word for word.

Talk with Me
Talk with me on cold dark nights
when the rain hits my window
And the thunder storms start
PLEASE TALK WITH ME
Talk to me about your thoughts
And I'll talk back
We will talk and talk all day
PLEASE TALK WITH ME

by Laura Begin from *Together Is Better,* COLLECTIONS 5

List and discuss their ideas. Then, using their list of ideas, establish a set of tips they could use when memorizing text for a word-by-word presentation.

Tips for Memorizing Text
- First, read the entire piece to get the overall meaning.
- Second, select phrases that go together, rather than trying to memorize single words.
- Third, read and repeat aloud each of the groupings of words or phrases one at a time.
- Fourth, repeat the piece in the order of beginning to end.
- Fifth, use gestures and vary the voice tone to match the text. This will help you remember the words and phrases.

Students could review Learning Strategy Card 48 for tips on how to memorize.

Invite pairs of students to use these tips to memorize the portion of "Talk with Me" or one of the poems in the selection. They can present their memorization to one another and discuss how the tips helped them. As a whole group, revisit the list of tips and make any revisions based on the students' experience.

Students could then work independently to memorize and present a favorite poem. The poems could be presented in small groups.

Assessment   See **Assess Learning**, page 127.

LINK TO CURRICULUM

Language Arts

Audio-Tape a Poem

Students could choose one of the poems from this selection or another they are familiar with to prepare for an audio presentation. Suggest that they practise reading their poem aloud, using expression and variety in their tone, pitch, and pace. Encourage them to read it aloud to several classmates and ask for their suggestions. For the taping, the students might want to play background music that is appropriate to enhance the words of the poem.

The students could put their readings on the same tape, which could be loaned to other classes for their listening pleasure.

Social Studies

Discuss Solutions for Problems

Have the students reread the poem, "To You," and concentrate on these two key phrases:
To sit and learn about the world
Outside our world of here and now—
Our problem world—
Help me to make
Our world anew.

Interested students could discuss and identify some of the problems occurring in our world. They may wish to organize their ideas around themes such as the environment, wars, racism, poverty, and so on. Then, in small groups, students could choose a particular theme and decide on a specific topic within the theme to discuss. For example, under the theme of the environment, they might talk about dumping garbage in the ocean, underground disposal of harmful chemicals, what to do about radioactive wastes, and so on.

Encourage them to describe the problem and its effects on others and to generate ways the problem might be dealt with or solved. Each group could share their problem and solution(s) with the larger group.

Science

Find Out About Dreams and Dreaming

Students can work in pairs to find information about people's and animals' dreams and other interesting facts about dreaming. They could consider questions like the following to help guide their investigation.
– How often do we dream?
– Do animals dream? All animals? Do we know what they dream about?
– Do babies dream?
– What happens to your brain and your body during dreams?
– How do scientists learn about dreaming?
– Why do we dream?

Have the pairs of students consolidate and organize their research information on one large fact sheet to share with their classmates. Encourage them to include diagrams, illustrations, and personal comments to add interest and variety to their fact sheet.

The Arts

Make a Dream Catcher

Blackline Masters 20 and 21

Explain to the students that it is a belief of some First Nations peoples that bad dreams can be caught in the web of a dream catcher and never become part of the sleeper's dreams. Only good and pleasant dreams are allowed through the catcher's web and into the dreams of the sleeper.

Interested students can follow the instructions on Blackline Masters 20 and 21, *Make A Dream Catcher*, to make a dream catcher for themselves or a special friend.

Blackline Master 20

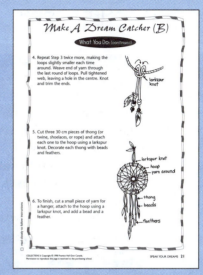

Blackline Master 21

Assess Learning

Assessment

Oral Communication (see p. 124)

Choose five to six students at a time to work within a **group conference** to assess how well they were able to utilize the tips when memorizing their selection and what they learned from the experience. For each of the students:

– Ask them to choose one or two of the tips that proved to be most helpful to them.
– Ask them to discuss which of the tips were not successful for them.
– Discuss what they would do differently when memorizing another selection at another time.
– Have them share what advice they would give to someone new at memorizing printed material.

> **The Smile** — *a poem*
>
> **Sign Language** — *a report*

LINK TO THE THEME

After reading the selections independently, the students could form small groups to
- talk about what all the writing has in common.
- discuss the main theme of each piece and whether the format chosen by the author fits the theme.
- tell which piece of writing they preferred and why.

LINK TO THE WRITING PROCESS

Write a Report

Reread the report "Sign Language" with the students, and then talk about its structure, pointing out that it is a report written in one paragraph. Discuss the features of the paragraph, noting that it has:
- an introduction that introduces the topic of sign language (first two sentences)
- detail sentences that tell more about the topic
- a conclusion that makes a summary statement about the topic (last sentence)

Point out to the students that the structure of this one-paragraph report parallels the structure of a multi-paragraph report, which usually has an introductory paragraph, a number of paragraphs that develop details about the topic, and a concluding paragraph.

Students could then choose a topic related to communication to research, and then write a one-paragraph report.

Language Workshop — Style
- use correctly the conventions of spelling

Blackline Master 22

Teach/Explore/Discover

Reread the poem, "The Smile," with the students and ask them to find pairs of rhyming words and jot them on the board. Talk about how the word pairs have the same sound and the same number of syllables, although some have different spelling patterns.

Begin a class chart of rhyming words by using words from the poem. Ask the students to brainstorm others they know that have the same sound and add these to the chart.

Practise/Apply

Students could
- complete Blackline Master 22, *Rhyming Words*.
- look for unusual or interesting rhyming words to add to the chart.

Blackline Master 22

LINK TO THE WRITER

Ask the students to identify the types of writing in the selection. Discuss how Taryn Green chose a poetry form with rhyming words to express her feelings about smiling, and Tamzin El-Fityani wrote a report to provide information about the language of the deaf.

Students can brainstorm and record different types of writing that they can use to express feelings and/or information about a topic, and save them for future writing projects.

STUDENT WRITING

Using the Genre Books and Novels

Learning Expectations

Students will

1. Read a variety of fiction and non-fiction materials for different purposes

2. Explain their interpretation of a written work, supporting it with evidence from the work and from their own knowledge and experience

3. Use their knowledge of the characteristics of different forms of writing to select the appropriate materials for a specific purpose

Approaching the Books

- Arrange the students in four groups, with each group reading a different book.
- Students could preview the books to self-select the one that they would like to read or read the book that best fits their reading level (see pages 6–7).
- Following the book "study," the groups could exchange books and read the other books as part of personal reading if they wish.

PACING TIP

Use the books as a group book exploration and study during the last two weeks of the unit.

Strategies for Book Connections and Study

Literature Response Journal

Students can write in their journals following the first reading or keep notes throughout the reading experience.

Suggest that they write
- impressions about the story or the characters.
- questions about parts they didn't understand.
- notes about things that surprised them.

Reading Workshop

Following the first reading, ask students who read the same book to form small workshop groups. They could begin by
- talking about their favorite parts of the book.
- posing questions about parts they didn't understand or that surprised them.

Guide each group to develop a collaborative plan for focusing their workshops over a few days.

Our Reading Workshop Plan

Day 1 – Discuss characters
- Who are they?
- What are they like?
- Who do they remind us of?

Day 2 – Discuss plot
- What surprised us in the plot?
- Did the plot turn out the way we thought it would?

- How would we change the plot?

Day 3 – Share reactions
- We'll take turns sharing and discussing together our journal notes.

Day 4 – Read aloud our favorite parts

The Reader Response activities in each teaching plan provide other ideas for workshops.

Whale Brother

Young Omu wants to become a great carver, but he must first find the *garrtsiluni,* the stillness. He must learn to see the animal in the bone so he can set it free when he carves. This picture book by Barbara Steiner relates most closely to the topic focus of communicating/expressing yourself through the arts (see pages 6-7).

INTRODUCING THE BOOK
Write About Learning Experiences

Ask the students to write in their journals about a time when they wanted to learn to do something very much, but found it very difficult. They might focus on

- how they felt as they struggled to learn
- what kinds of things they did to learn
- whether they received encouragement to continue from their friends/family
- whether they finally succeeded, and if so, how/why
- whether they stopped trying, and if so, why

Recall "Carving a Totem Pole"

Ask the students to skim "Carving a Totem Pole" (*Off the Page,* p. 16) to find evidence that Norman Tait felt spiritually and emotionally connected to his work. Discuss other artists they read about in the unit who also felt a strong connection to their work. Then ask the students to think about some of the best artistic works they have produced and to talk about if/how they felt linked in some way to the art.

CONNECTING WITH THE BOOK
Explore Book Features

Prior to reading, ask the students to look at the book and note features such as the following:

- the cover and title page
- copyright information
- the author's and illustrator's dedications
- the illustrations
- the information about the author and the illustrator at the back

Invite the students to predict what they think will happen in the story after they read the short summary and look at the illustrations.

Reading Focus

Using the **read and paraphrase** strategy, pairs of students can take turns reading parts of the story aloud and orally summarizing the story events. **(See Activity 1.)**

> Activities on the next two pages serve as guides to focus students' reading and response. The pages can be duplicated and made into transparencies, response sheets, or activity cards.

A SUGGESTED APPROACH TO READING THE BOOKS

Provide time for at least two readings:

First Reading

The main goal of the first reading is to provide students with a satisfying reading experience along with a general understanding of the book.

Students who are at the **fluent stage** could read the entire text on their own, pausing to discuss portions of the text as they wish.

Students who would benefit from more **guidance** could use the strategy targeted for the selection.

Further Readings

As students engage in further readings, they will deepen and extend their understanding and appreciation through a more detailed exploration of the book.

Read *Whale Brother*

With a partner, take turns reading parts of the story aloud. After reading your part,

• tell what happened in the story

• ask your partner to add any important details that you missed

Then jot any questions or thoughts you and your partner have about the part. After reading the whole story, discuss your questions and thoughts with another pair of students.

Read	Questions and Thoughts We Have
Read to "He forgot his problem of making a bone come alive."	
Read to "So, early each morning, he paddled to his secret place."	
Read to "Had his friends returned to the ocean?"	
Read to "Aja, I am a brother to the sea."	
Read to "I have great joy."	
Read to the end of the story.	

Whale Brother ☐ read a variety of fiction and non-fiction materials for different purposes

READER RESPONSE

 Research Killer Whales

Locate resources that provide information about killer whales. Choose those facts you find the most interesting and organize them in a one-page fact sheet. Add diagrams or pictures to your fact sheet. Then compare your sheet with those of other students.

Whale Brother

 Choral Read the Songs

With a group of classmates, reread the songs that Omu wrote. Talk about the messages he was conveying and the mood of each of them. Then choose a few to choral read. You might want to read the songs all together as a group or have some lines read by individuals. After you have practised, present your choral readings to the class.

Whale Brother

 Make a Soap Carving

Choose an animal that is special to you. Think about how it looks and how it moves. Think about its characteristics that you would like to show. Use a large bar of soap and carve the animal.

Then write a short piece on a file card explaining why you chose the animal and what you were trying to show. Display your carving and card in your classroom.

Whale Brother

 Read Other Inuit Stories

Choose a story to read that tells about the way of life and beliefs of the Inuit people. Or choose an Inuit tale to read. When you are finished reading, prepare a book talk to share the story with your classmates. These are some books you can look for.

A Promise Is a Promise
Robert Munsch and Michael Kusugak

Baseball Bats for Christmas
Michael Kusugak

Northern Lights the Soccer Trails
Michael Kusugak

Hide and Sneak
Michael Kusugak

Whale Brother

 Write a Profile of the Author

Find out more about the author, Barbara Steiner, and write a profile about her. You might start with questions like these.

• Why did she become an author?

• How does her involvement with Greenpeace and the Audubon Society influence her writing?

• What other books has she written?

Think about different ways you could get information, such as writing or faxing the publisher or the author herself, and using the Internet and printed reference materials about published books and authors.

Whale Brother

Kids Rule the Internet: The Ultimate Guide

This guide by Jason Page presents information about a multitude of aspects of the Internet in a way that is easy to understand and humorous. This book relates most closely to the topic focus of communicating through mass media (see pages 6-7).

INTRODUCING THE BOOK

Check on Experience

With the students, discuss the experiences they have had with the Internet: where they have used it/watched it being used, what they have used it for, ..., . Make a list of some of the Internet terms they are familiar with and talk about what they mean.

Ask the students to rate their experience with the Internet as "considerable, some, minimal, or none." This information can be used for the reading focus activity and some reader response activities.

Recall "Get Set for the Net!"

Ask the students to skim the article "Get Set for the Net!" (*Off the Page*, p. 28) to help them recall what information it provided about the Internet: its history, features, cyberspace, and the I-Way. Suggest that they keep this background information in mind as they read *Kids Rule the Internet: The Ultimate Guide*.

CONNECTING WITH THE BOOK

Explore Book Features

Prior to reading, ask students to look at the book and note features such as the following:
• the cover with the title and cartoon-type art

• the dedication, note of appreciation, and title page, with their touch of humor
• copyright information, including place of publication
• contents page, noting the topics that are covered
• information on the back cover

Discuss whether a book about the Internet produced in England can be useful in Canada.

Reading Focus

Note: The strategy suggested here may need to be adapted to fit your students' experience and interest, and classroom access to the Internet.

Students can use the **read, paraphrase, and teach** strategy to read certain sections of the guide, paraphrase what they learn, and teach that material to classmates. **(See Activity 1.)**

First, however, have all the students read and discuss the "Read Me File" chapter on pages 6 to 8 to familiarize themselves with the way the book works. To help with their understanding of the vocabulary of the Internet, they can also read the chapters entitled "TLAs and ETLAs" and "Netspeak" and individually list ten new terms they learned.

> Activities on the next two pages serve as guides to focus students' reading and response. The pages can be duplicated and made into transparencies, response sheets, or activity cards.

Read *Kids Rule the Internet: The Ultimate Guide*

This kids' guide to the Internet tells you how to get on the Net and explains all the neat things you can do while you're surfing. Some of these surfing activities are listed on the back cover of the book. Choose two of these topics that interest you. Check the contents page and write down the titles of the chapters and the page numbers that you think are about your two topics. You may have to skim through parts of the book to determine which chapters deal with your topics.

Now form a small group with classmates who are interested in reading about one of the topics you chose.

Things To Do With Your Group

☐ read your chapter(s) of the book

☐ study the diagrams and/or charts

☐ talk about what you've read and ask questions about things you don't understand

☐ try the activities

☐ plan and give an oral presentation to the whole group that will tell what you learned about the topic. Include charts, drawings, and demonstrations.

If there is time, you may want to work with another group to find out about your other topic of interest.

Kids Rule the Internet

☐ use their knowledge of the characteristics of different forms of writing to select the appropriate materials for a specific purpose

READER RESPONSE

 Create a Signature, Message, or Picture

Read pages 28 and 38 to 41 to get some ideas about how to use characters on the keyboard to create interesting signatures, messages, or pictures. Try some of these on the computer. Then use your imagination to create some of your own. Here are some things you can do.

• create a design for your name and a few friends' names

• write a computer message to someone and include some emoticons

  Examples (turn them to see the faces): :–) ;–) >:–(

• draw a picture using keyboard characters

• design a "sig" for yourself that includes your name and "nick," snail mail address, and your telephone number

Kids Rule the Internet

Share Humorous Parts

Skim through parts of the guide you have read, and with a piece of paper or sticky note, mark several parts you thought were humorous. Get together with a partner and take turns reading these parts to one another. Talk about the type of humor the author uses.

Kids Rule the Internet

Hold a Debate

Read the chapter called "Adults Only." Think about the problem of kids coming across undesirable material such as rude pictures, information on drugs, and how to make bombs. Write a statement that expresses a point of view about this area, for example:

> The Internet should be censored so nothing bad is on it.

> Every kid should have access to everything on the Internet.

> Only parents should be able to tell their children what they can or cannot access on the Internet.

Then get together with a group of students and hold a debate about your statement or about a statement another classmate came up with.

Kids Rule the Internet

Plan a Kids' Cybercafe

On page 31, you can read about cybercafes in England. Think about what you would want in a cybercafe for kids in your community. What would your menu be? How would you have the tables, computers, food counter, and so on arranged? What other things would you have in your cafe? What would you call it? Make a drawing or a 3-dimensional model of your kids' cybercafe.

Kids Rule the Internet

Have Fun with Spelling

Look back on pages 6 and 7 to note the odd way that BoTom spells some words. Write down the words you see here and determine the pattern for his odd way of spelling. List other words from the guide or ones you can think of that could be spelled with the same patterns.

Make a list of words you would spell differently if you were making up your own spelling rules. Group your words according to patterns. Beside your odd spellings, write the words in color with their correct spelling.

Kids Rule the Internet

Journey

In this novel by Patricia MacLachlan, a young boy struggles to understand why his mother has left him and his sister, Cat. Journey searches through old photographs, and participates in his grandfather's new hobby of photography in an attempt to come to grips with his life. This novel relates most closely to the topic focuses of communicating/expressing yourself through the arts and communicating in person (see pages 6-7).

INTRODUCING THE BOOK

Write About a Personal Experience

Ask the students to recall a time when a grandparent, other older family member, or an older friend helped them work through a problem or overcome a challenge. Invite them to write about it in their journals. Encourage them to include details that tell about their feelings and how the experiences or knowledge of the other person helped them.

Recall "Dancing the Cotton-Eyed Joe"

Ask the students to think back on the story, "Dancing the Cotton-Eyed Joe" (*Off the Page*, p. 69), to recall Alice, the young blind girl. Have them skim the story to find things that she said or did that show how she coped with her own personal challenge of being blind.

In small groups, invite the students to share personal experiences where a person they know or themselves had to deal with a difficult challenge, such as an illness, the loss of a loved one, or an accident, and discuss what they or others did to cope with the situation.

CONNECTING WITH THE BOOK

Explore Book Features

Prior to reading, ask the students to look over the book and note features such as the following:
• the title and copyright pages
• the dedication and quotes
• the accolades " Praise for *Journey*"
• the text preceding chapter one
• the organization of the novel, noting that there are 13 chapters

Invite students to talk about their first thoughts or impressions about the book.

Reading Focus

Students can use the **read and connect** strategy to read the novel independently or with a partner, stopping at the end of sections to make personal connections with the story. **(See Activity 1.)**

> Activities on the next two pages serve as guides to focus students' reading and response. The pages can be duplicated and made into transparencies, response sheets, or activity cards.

Read *Journey*

In this novel, Journey's mother leaves him and his sister with their grandparents. The story tells how those left behind learn to deal with this, each in their own way.

On your own or with a partner, read each section of the novel. Then make an entry in your literature response journal telling what you thought about after reading the section. Choose one of the sentence starters and one sentence frame to guide each of your responses. At the end of each section, share your thoughts with a partner.

Sections:	**Sentence Starters:**
1. Chapters One and Two	I think …
2. Chapters Three and Four	I wonder …
3. Chapter Five	I noticed …
4. Chapter Six	I predict …
5. Chapter Seven	I feel …
6. Chapter Eight	I don't understand …
7. Chapter Nine	I enjoyed …
8. Chapters Ten and Eleven	I disagree …
9. Chapters Twelve and Thirteen	

Sentence Frames:

1. What impressed me in this chapter/section was_____.

2. _____reminds me of _____because_____

_____

3. The author could have_____.

4. I felt _____ about_____

because_____.

Journey   ☐ explain their interpretation of a written work, supporting it with
                                evidence from the work and from their own knowledge and experience

READER RESPONSE

 Read Other Books by Patricia MacLachlan

Patricia MacLachlan has written several other books. Find some of these books in your school library or public library and choose one to read. Then write a comparison, telling how the book you read and *Journey* are the same and how they are different. Share your ideas with your classmates, either by reading or posting your writing.

Journey

 Illustrate Story Events

Imagine that you are Journey and you are selecting special photos for a photo album. Choose four to six events or incidents from the story that you think Journey would want in his album. Draw a "photo" for each event. Arrange and glue the photos on pieces of paper to make your photo album. Write a caption for each of the photos.

Journey

 Create a Character Map

Choose a character from the story and make a character trait map that describes the character. Be sure to include evidence from the novel that supports the traits you think your character has. Share your map with some classmates.

Journey

 Write Similes

Skim through the novel to find similes that the author uses to describe things. List these in your journal. For each one, write other similes that would provide different "pictures" for the reader.

the baby's laughter fell like sunlight across the room

the baby's laughter tinkled like wind chimes in a breeze

the baby's laughter floated like a bird's song in the air

Journey

 Make a Personal Photo Album

Look through photographs of your own and/or your family's to find ones that show something important in your life—an event or celebration, friends/family, an accomplishment, … . Choose 10 or 12, and arrange them in chronological order in an album. (You can make the album yourself using heavy paper or cardboard for mounting the photos.)

Share your album with a friend or your family and talk about why you chose the photos you did.

Journey

Coast to Coast

In this novel by Betsy Byars, Birch joins her grandfather in an adventurous flight across the United States in his antique Piper Cub. Through their conversations, messages in poetry, and technological means of communication, Birch learns about her grandfather's thoughts and dreams, about navigation, and about her family's history. This novel relates in some way to each of the topic focuses: communicating through the arts, mass media, and in person (see pages 6-7).

INTRODUCING THE BOOK

Make an Airplane Research Centre

Ask the students to gather materials such as pictures, books, magazines, CD-ROMs, ..., that tell about different kinds/types of planes over the years. These materials can be arranged in an area of the room where students can go to browse and do research during the time they are involved with this novel and its activities.

Recall "Carving a Totem Pole"

Have the students recall how, in the article "Carving a Totem Pole" (*Off the Page*, p. 16), the author explains that oral stories and those carved in totem poles are an important way of learning about family history. Ask the students to think about and discuss ways that their families' histories are passed on from generation to generation. Then tell them that family history is one of the threads in the story *Coast to Coast,* and ask them to watch for this as they read the novel.

CONNECTING WITH THE BOOK

Explore Book Features

Prior to reading, ask students to look at the book and note features such as the following:
• the cover with its title and picture
• reviewers' praise
• list of other Yearling books including some by Betsy Byars
• the map of the route across the United States
• picture and facing title page
• copyright information and dedication
• contents page
• information about the author following the last chapter
• introduction to the story on the back cover

Talk with students about the expectations set up by the reviewers' praise and the information on the back cover. Also discuss what is meant by the note about coverless books on the copyright page.

Reading Focus

Students can use a **read and reflect** strategy to read the novel independently in sections and note important events/points. **(See Activity 1.)**

> Activities on the next two pages serve as guides to focus students' reading and response. The pages can be duplicated and made into transparencies, response sheets, or activity cards.

Read *Coast to Coast*

This novel has two story lines. It tells about the adventures of Birch and her grandfather as they travel across the United States in his antique Piper J-3 Cub plane. It also tells of Birch's search to find out more about her family and to discover the meaning of a poem written by her grandmother.

Read the story in these sections.

Chapters 1–3   Chapters 11–14

Chapters 4–7   Chapters 15–19

Chapters 8–10   Chapters 20–23

Make a chart like the one below, to fill out as you read each of the sections. Stop at the end of each section to jot down the most important things that happened for each story line. The first section has been started for you.

Chapters to read	Important points about flying/the flight	Important points about the poem/ family history
1 to 3	— Pop going to sell plane — Pop talks about his dream to fly coast to coast — Birch talks Pop into taking her up in the plane for the first time and wanted to fly to be free — Pop flew in the war	— Birch discovers grandma's poems in attic, reads love poems and birth poem — talks to Pop, learns nothing about poem, finds out Pop was very poor
4 to 7		
8 to 10		

When you've finished the novel, share your chart with a partner and compare the points you put in the chart.

Coast to Coast   ☐ read a variety of fiction and non-fiction materials for different purposes

READER RESPONSE

 Make a Story Map

Use the notes you made while reading the story to help you make a story map. You can choose to map either the main events related to the flight across the United States, or the events related to Birch's search for the meaning of the poem. In your story map, include these headings: title, author, settings, characters, problem, events, solution.

Coast to Coast

3 Write and Answer Questions

Think back on the story and write six questions about it. Write two questions each of these different types:

Type of Question	Example
• the answers are right there in the story	What did Pop do in the war?
• you can figure out the answer based on information in the text	How did Pop feel about_____? How do you know?
• you need to make a judgement or decision	Do you think it was right for Birch to _____? Why?

Exchange questions with a partner to answer. Then share and discuss your answers to each other's questions.

Coast to Coast

 ## 4 Make Airplane Cards

Use a variety of pictures, books, magazines, or CD-ROMs for information to make at least two airplane cards. On the front of the card, draw and color a picture of the plane. On the back, provide important and interesting information about the plane. Organize your information under headings. Put your cards together with ones other students make and display them in the school or classroom library.

Coast to Coast

 ## 5 Plan a Flight Across Canada

With a partner, skim through the story to find out approximately how far Birch and Pop could travel on a tank full of gas during ideal conditions. Using this information, plan a similar trip across Canada in the same plane. Show the route of your flight on a map. You can indicate where you will stop each night and places you will pass over, just like the map for Birch and Pop's flight.

Coast to Coast

 ## 6 Web Ways of Communicating

Throughout the story, a number of ways of communicating thoughts and information are mentioned. Cut strips of paper about 6 cm x 2 cm. On them, write the different forms of communication you can find in the story.

Move the strips about into categories, such as the arts, technology, in person, or others you can think of. When you are satisfied with the way you have the strips organized, copy the groupings onto a piece of paper in the form of a web.

Coast to Coast

Concluding Connections and Study for the Genre Books and Novels

1. Share Small Group Learnings

Provide time for each book connection and study group to
- share their book, through a book talk or dramatization.
- lead a discussion on the ideas and topics in the book.
- tell how their book connects to the *Off the Page* anthology selections and to the ideas encountered in the unit.
- do an oral reading of a section of the book.
- share some of their Reader Response activities.

2. Hold a Whole Class Conversation

Help the students synthesize and summarize the understandings they have about their books by choosing questions similar to the following ones. Encourage responses to each question from all members of all of the book connections and study groups.

Questions for discussion

- Did you like the title the author chose for the book? Why? Why not? What title would you have chosen?
- Who is the main character(s)? What means of communication did the character(s) use?
- What do you think the author(s) is trying to tell you by writing the book? Why do you think so?
- If you could change any part of the book, what would it be? Why? What change(s) would you make?
- What personal connections can you make to the events, activities, or characters in the book?

You might choose one question a day for a period of five days to either begin or end the class. Post the questions a day ahead of time so students can prepare their ideas and draw upon specific references in their respective books.

3. Make a Personal Response

Provide prompts such as the following for the students. They could
- write about what type of book it is and describe features that make it a fiction or non-fiction book.
- choose a main character from a book and make a few journal entries as if they were that character relating particular events or reflecting on something from the book.
- make a set of question-and-answer cards about the book and create a game to play with other students.
- design a new back cover for the book with such features as a summary, praise from student reviewers, and/or notes about the author/illustrator.
- write a newspaper article telling about an incident in the book.
- create a poster that will entice others to read the book and hang the poster in the classroom, hallway, or school library.

The students' responses could be assessed and placed in their portfolios as one record of their understanding of the book.

Assess the Unit

Throughout the unit, there are many opportunities for ongoing assessment and celebration of what students have learned and accomplished in guided mini-lessons and in individual or small group activities.

Ongoing Observations

Consolidate ongoing observations that you have noted for each student using the "Ongoing Assessment" boxes, your observation of literature discussions, group discussions, and so on.

Unit Assessment Checklist

Use the *Assess Working Style and Attitudes Assessment Master* (*Assessment Handbook*) to help you assess performance on attitudes. Use *Appendix 1* (pp. 174-175) in this book to help you assess and record student performance.

Gather and Record Assessment Information and Data

ASSESSMENT SUGGESTIONS

The *COLLECTIONS 6 Assessment Handbook* contains many suggestions and reproducible forms to assist with assessment and evaluation.

1. Reading

Use the **Off the Page** *Reading Passages Assessment Masters* (*Assessment Handbook*). Students can read and respond to either or both of the passages. The Handbook describes how to choose the passages, how to conduct the activity, and criteria for scoring.

2. Writing

Students could submit one piece of writing of their choice for assessment.

Procedures and criteria for assessing the writing can be found in the *Assessment Handbook*.

3. Sample of Students' Learning for Portfolios

Review and assess learning records such as the following:
• logs of books students have read (*Reading Log Master, Assessment Handbook*)
• spelling and vocabulary pretests and post tests
• writing portfolios, including pieces of writing started or completed
• displays, models, scientific diagrams, and artwork
• research reports ▶

- webs, charts, notes crafted by students
- tapes of oral reading, oral presentations, or reports
- assignments of work or worksheets demonstrating performance on specific literacy tasks (such as those identified in "Assess Learning" activities noted throughout the unit)

Choose samples that will remain in the assessment portfolio as a record of student performance on the unit. The *Portfolio Checklist Master* in the *Assessment Handbook* may help you synthesize your assessment of students' work samples.

4. Self-Assessment

Students could
- **write in their learning logs** what they have learned about communicating—through the arts, through mass media, and in person.
- **write a self-assessment report or "can do" list** to describe what they have learned. They might benefit from using the *Thinking Back on the Unit Assessment Master* (*Assessment Handbook*) containing prompts or lead-in phrases to help them focus on aspects of their learning.

They can use what they have prepared to help them plan what skills they need to work on in the next unit.

5. Teacher-Student Conferences

Throughout the unit, take opportunities to talk with individual students to see how they are progressing in personal reading and writing. Use or adapt
- *Questions to Guide a Personal Reading Conference Assessment Master* (*Assessment Handbook*) to help you conduct a **reading conference.**
- *Questions to Guide a Personal Writing Conference Assessment Master* (*Assessment Handbook*) to help you conduct a **writing conference.**

AT THE END OF AN ACTIVITY OR UNIT

My Self-Assessment Report

I liked the story called "Fax Facts" because my dad has an office at home and he has a fax machine too. I laughed at how Barney went crazy with the fax machine! My dad showed me how the fax works but he told me that it's not a toy. I think it's cool how you can get something right away without having to wait for it to come in the mail!

Something that really made me laugh was the story, "Anti-Snore Machine." It reminded me of my house when my grandpa comes to stay over! He snores too and sometimes he snores really loud! The story is right! My grandma says all she has to do is to tell grandpa to turn over onto his side and, like magic, the snoring stops!

After I read the story called "Dancing the Cotton-Eyed Joe," I thought a lot about what it must be like to be blind. I never thought about it much before. For my research group, I talked to a lady at the CNIB. I learned a lot from her about how life is different for someone who is blind, but how it is very much the same too. I also learned this from the story.

My favorite activity was learning a new dance. I love to dance. I learned to dance to "Never on a Sunday." My sitter who is in high school came to teach the class. It's a line dance and it's a lot of fun! Now I hum the music that goes with it all the time.

I had trouble making my totem pole. I talked to my parents to try to find out different things about my family, and tried to think of pictures that would explain those stories. I found it very hard, but I did a pretty good job in the end.

Blackline Masters

Spelling Words Masters

Off the Page
Home Connections Newsletter

About the Unit

Our new unit in language arts is *Off the Page*. For the next month or so, we'll be talking, reading, and writing about messages that are communicated through the arts, mass media, and in person. As we work together, the students will have many opportunities to reflect on their experiences with messages through media such as carvings, photography, digital art, the Internet, as well as person-to-person contact.

You can help your child make the connection at home. Together, look through this newsletter and choose books to share and activities and homework projects to do.

Learning Goals

In this unit, your child will

- listen to, read, and talk about fiction and non-fiction selections related to communication in a variety of interesting ways
- write interviews, poems, scripts, and stories
- explore and use technology as a way of communicating with others and gaining information
- use and appreciate non-verbal communication
- learn to spell words from personal and class lists

BOOK BAG

These stories are about messages communicated in ways other than with "pencil and paper." Look for one or more of these books at your local library for your child to read or to share together.

- *The Acting Bug* by Kathyrn Ellis. Kate is thrilled when she gets a part in a TV series. Then she finds out her best friend has already turned it down.
- *Cartooning for Kids* by Marge Lightfoot. A helpful how-to book gives all the basics about creating cartoons.
- *Fun-tastic Collages* by Mark Thurman. Easy instructions about how to recycle every-day objects into dazzling designs.
- *The Magic Paintbrush* by Robin Muller. Nib, an orphan boy, is given a magic paintbrush that brings pictures to life.
- *Video* by Jackie Biel. A book about how video was invented and how it is used today.

A Family Movie Night

As a family, rent a video or attend a movie that is the screen version of a young person's novel. After the movie, talk about the characters and the story, and share parts that you each liked particularly well, and tell why. You might wish to get a copy of the book and compare the two.

Your child will be reading stories, articles, and poems about how messages are communicated through ways other than the traditional print text. Together, talk about a selection that your child likes and ask him/her to draw or tell about a favorite part.

Homemade Fun

Have a Discussion

Find a time when most of the family is together, and talk about questions such as:
- What creative talents do you see in members of your extended family? How have they been developed?
- What changes and developments have taken place in movie animation over time?
- What are the advantages and disadvantages to being on the Internet?
- How has technology like e-mail, the Internet, and the fax brought people closer together? Does it have other effects on the way people relate to one another?

Learn About Morphing and Digital Warping

This is something students in the classroom will be reading about. As a family, you might:
- locate information in magazines or books or on the Internet.
- view a cartoon, movie, or television commercial in which animators have used high-tech computer programs and techniques to produce special effects.
- try out some programs and techniques using available computer software programs.

Appreciate the Arts

Look in the entertainment section of your newspaper or on community bulletin boards to find an art exhibition, musical concert, dance program, or a theatre play you can attend with your child. After attending, talk about what messages the artists conveyed and what aspects appealed to each of you.

Homework Projects

Week 1 — Write About a Work of Art
Visit a local gallery or other art exhibit with a family member. Or, look through a number of art books. Choose one piece of art that you particularly like and make jot notes about it—what the piece is about/shows, the medium the artist used, the colors, the mood, ..., . Then write a short report about it using your jot notes. Also explain how the piece makes you feel and what it makes you think about.

Week 2 — Answer a Question
Ask at least five people for their opinion about the following question: What things can be done to protect the natural areas in our community? Tape-record their answers or write down what they say. Share their responses with some classmates. See if you can add any other ideas to theirs.

Week 3 — Make a High-Tech Dictionary
Skim through magazines, books, and newspapers to find and list high-tech terms. Write the terms in alphabetical order in a booklet. Provide a definition, and maybe an illustration, for each term. Here are some to get you started: network, surf the net, menu, and cyberspace.

Week 4 — Learn a Dance
Ask your family members to show you their favorite dances. They may like waltzes, polkas, the twist, and many others. Practise the dances with them. Then choose the one you like the best, learn to do it well, and share what you learned with some classmates.

Explore Computers and Communication Technology

To become familiar with some of the advances in computer technology, fax machines, video cameras, and so on, plan to make a few visits to a computer and/or office supply store, or attend a communications technology show or display with your child. Ask questions and take advantage of demonstrations and opportunities to try things out. There may be brochures you can take home to read and discuss.

Meeting Metaphors

Read this poem and underline the metaphors.

Hopes

Hold onto your hopes,
For if hopes fade away,
Life is a lame deer
That cannot run.

Stand close to your hopes
For when hope goes,
Life is a parched sea
Frozen with regrets.

A metaphor describes something by saying it is something else.

Complete each phrase with a metaphor.

1 Courage is _____

_____

2 Sadness is _____

_____

3 Excitement is _____

_____

4 Anger is _____

_____

Think about something in nature that you enjoy, like a rainbow or a meadow of wildflowers. Write sentences using metaphors to describe two of these things.

5 _____

_____

6 _____

_____

Look at a piece of your own writing. Find at least three places where you can add or change a metaphor to improve the piece. Share your improvements with a partner.

Follow Along Grid(1)

Use this grid to guide you as you read the biography of Wang Yani. At each stopping point, write your responses in your journal.

Read	Write
Read to "Her favorite music is Chinese music, Beethoven's Fifth Symphony, and works by Schubert and Mozart." (p. 11)	1. Describe some of the things Yani does to help her paint. 2. What techniques/methods does Yani use to paint? 3. How did Yani change artistically as she got older?
Read to "He added that he hopes to go back to his own painting when Yani turns eighteen." (p. 12)	4. What did you learn about Yani's father? 5. What else did you learn about Yani and how she paints?
Read to "He adds that it is important to keep that guidance within the boundaries of the child's stage of development." (p. 14)	6. Yani's father guided her growth as an artist in a variety of ways. Describe some of the things he has done.
Read to the end of the biography.	7. What does this last section tell you about Yani? About her father?

Make webs of words and phrases to describe Yani and her father.

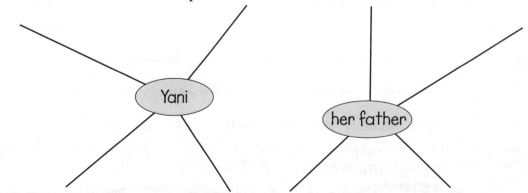

Main and Supporting Details

Read each paragraph and highlight both the main and the supporting details. Use a different color for the two kinds of details.

So Inuit live off the land—and that means we hunt animals for food. In our language, the wild animals we hunt are not called *game*. They are not to be played with. They are called *nirjutit,* which means " food." We do not hunt caribou for prize antlers, we do not play with fish on a line, we do not mount animals' heads to show them off, and we do not hunt polar bears for sport. We are not allowed to waste meat of any kind. Take what you need and leave the animals alone—that's the rule.

by Michael Kusugak

Dr. von Frish figured out how bees send their messages. They dance! He called it the "waggle" dance. The pattern of the bee's dance is a figure eight. She repeats it over and over again as her sister bees watch. The most important part of the dance is the straight run through the middle of the figure eight. That shows the direction from the hive to the food. If the bee is dancing outside the hive on a flat surface, she lines up with the sun, then turns to point toward the food. If the bee is inside, on the wall of the dark hive, her head points up, as if the sun were overhead. Then she turns right or left to show where the food is.

adapted from "Dancing Bees" by Margery Facklam

The next day is the pole raising. Tait family members and other Nisga'a arrive early. All of them bring button blankets and other ceremonial items such as frontlets, rattles, and talking sticks. Although Norman's mind is full of details about the difficult pole raising, he still takes time to give his niece a reassuring hug.

from "Carving a Totem Pole" by Vickie Jensen

Share and discuss your work with a partner. Look at the similarities and differences in your choice of main and supporting details in these paragraphs.

Work with Apostrophes

Write a sentence using the correct form of the possessive for each of the following. The first one has been done for you.

1 Dat owns a set of drums
Dat's drums were stored in the basement.

2 the artists presented a fine display
_____
_____

3 the rock band put on a performance
_____
_____

4 the shouts of the children could be heard
_____
_____

5 Mrs. Wong and Shirley own a music store together
_____
_____

6 Josh and Ali each own a bike
_____
_____

Choose a topic and write a short paragraph about it, using as many possessives as you can. Share your paragraph and the sentences you wrote above with a friend. Check to see if you each wrote the possessives correctly.

_____
_____
_____
_____
_____
_____

Look through some of your own writing pieces to find where you used possessives. Did you punctuate them correctly?

Taking A Photograph

Use this grid to help you plan your photographs. Jot notes for each of the subheadings. Then sketch a picture of what your photographs should look like.

Photo One:

	Sketch:
Subject: Setting: Point of View/Angle: Lighting:	

Photo Two:

	Sketch:
Subject: Setting: Point of View/Angle: Lighting:	

Photo Three:

	Sketch:
Subject: Setting: Point of View/Angle: Lighting:	

Compare the results of your photos with other classmates and discuss what worked well and what did not.

Write with Description

Rewrite these sentences. Use descriptive language.

1. The wind blew through the trees, making them sway.

_____

_____

2. Kristie stood in the wings, waiting for her turn to go on stage.

_____

_____

3. As I looked at the painting, a feeling of excitement came over me.

_____

_____

4. Taylor sat on the rock looking across the meadow of flowers.

_____

_____

Edit or rewrite this paragraph to add vivid and descriptive language that shows how the author really feels about running.

I love to run. It makes me feel great. When I run, my mind goes for a rest and I sure need that now and again. The best thing about running is that you are in control and doing good things for your body. I begin with some stretching and then move onto a fast paced walk. In no time I am running on the pavement. And every step reminds me of neat things. You should try running. It's great!

_____

_____

_____

_____

_____

Choose your own topic and compose a paragraph that really shows your feelings and attitude about the topic.

Exchange your writing with a partner. Read your partner's writing carefully and provide feedback about what you like about her or his use of vivid language. As well, suggest places where more descriptive language could be used.

Follow Along Grid (2)

Read the selection in sections and do the activities on your own. Then share your ideas with a partner.

Read this section	Do these things
Read the introduction on page 28.	1. Draw a spider web showing the strands of silk, a spider, and the flies caught in it. Show how the Internet is like a spider web by labelling the parts that would correspond to the telephone lines, the computers, and information.
Read "History of a Hooked-Up World," pages 28-31.	2. Beside the names of the following people, write a sentence telling about their contributions to communication technology. • Samuel Morse • Christopher Stokes • Thomas A. Edison • Guglielmo Marconi
Read "Reality Byte" and "Famous First Words," page 32.	3. List two interesting things you learned here. 4. Check to see how you did on the quiz "Famous First Words."
Read "Life Is a Highway" (page 32) to the end of the article.	5. Write a definition for "cyberspace" and tell what you need to get there. 6. Follow the path of the I-Way with your finger, stopping at each icon along the way and reading the definitions of the icons to make sure you understand the importance of each aspect of the I-Way.

Follow Along Grid (3)

Use this grid to guide you in reading and thinking about the story. At each stopping point, write the answers to the questions. Answer the questions at the end, and then share all your answers with a partner.

Read	Think and Jot Down
Read from the beginning of the story to "'I'm the one who taught you to program the VCR, remember?'" (top of page 47) to find out about Barney's new fax machine.	**1** List the four uses Barney has already found for the new fax machine. **2** Tell about something in your own experience you are reminded of by something one of the characters says, thinks, or does.
Read to the bottom of page 47, "... so in one night I got twenty-two faxes!" to find out about the problem that is developing.	**3** Describe how you think Hatch is feeling. Tell about a time when you felt like that. **4** What do you think is going to happen next? What makes you think that?
Read to the end of the story to see if your prediction was right.	**5** List five words that describe how you think Barney felt when he made the discovery about the words to the song. **6** Tell about a situation of yours, or one in a book or movie, that you were reminded of when this happened to Barney.

 7 What do you think about the way Hatch handled the whole situation?

_____

_____

 8 What do you think Barney thought about while he was bagging groceries?

_____

_____

Sentence Fragments

Read the sentences below and decide whether or not they express a complete thought. Then, on the line, write **"sentence"** or **"fragment."** Rewrite the fragments into complete sentences.

> A **sentence** expresses a complete thought and has both a subject and a predicate. A sentence **fragment** only expresses part of a thought and is missing either a subject or a predicate.

1 Hatch looked worried. _____

2 They faxed me instructions for raising rabbits. _____

3 The one who taught you to program the VCR. _____

4 A weather service that updates forecasts often. _____

_____

_____

_____

Sentence fragments are often used in dialogue because that's the way people talk. In the dialogue below, underline the sentence fragments.

5 "Practise? Right now?" questioned Barney. "I have to wait for these faxes to come in."

6 "You have to learn four verses of the song." said Hatch. "Four verses!"

7 "Oh, oh! Trouble! I've got the wrong fax taped onto my guitar!" Barney exclaimed to himself.

8 "You'll have to get a job to pay off your portion of the telephone bill," Father said in a stern voice. "Imagine, thirty dollars in fax bills!"

 Think about a recent incident that happened to you or that you know about and write a short story about it. Include as much dialogue among the characters as possible. Use sentence fragments in the dialogue whenever it seems like the most natural way to have the characters speak. Share your story with a partner.

Talk It Up

Use this sheet as a guide to prepare your speech.

1. I have chosen to speak about _____

   It is important because _____

2. The audience I will give my speech to is _____

   I will make the topic interesting for them by _____

   _____

   Their knowledge of this topic is   limited   average   great   varied

3. Points I know already about this topic:

   •

   •

   •

4. Areas I need to research:

   •

   •

   •

5. Places, people, and materials I can use to do my research:

   •

   •

   •

6. I will organize my speech by

   ☐ sub-topic   ☐ questions
   ☐ chronological order   ☐ other: _____

7. I will begin in an interesting way with a

   ☐ story   ☐ statement
   ☐ question   ☐ other: _____

8. I will end by tying things together with a

   ☐ summary statement   ☐ joke
   ☐ story   ☐ moral
                                   ☐ other: _____

9. I will include gestures/charts/illustrations in these places.

   •

   •

   •

Interesting Ways To Begin

Read the following story beginnings. Jot what they tell you about the story—characters, setting, mood, and/or plot.

1. Standing at the bus stop just in front of Henry was a girl with a cabbage tied to her head.
   (from *The Mystical Beast* by Alison Farthing)

2. The island of Gont, a single mountain that lifts its peak a mile above the storm-racked Northeast Sea, is a land famous for wizards.
   (from *A Wizard of Earthsea* by Ursula K. LeGuin)

3. Let me tell you what happened after I saw the weird blue lights.
   (from *Invasion of the Blue Lights* by Ruth Glick)

Read the following story opening. Rewrite it three different ways: (a) to give more information about "she"; (b) to set a scary mood; (c) to give some details of the setting.

4. She stood at the door of the house, listening to the music playing inside. She lifted her hand to knock.

   (a) _____
   _____

   (b) _____
   _____

   (c) _____
   _____

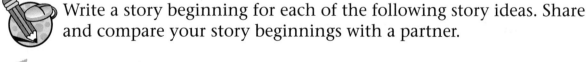 Write a story beginning for each of the following story ideas. Share and compare your story beginnings with a partner.

5. (a) a surprise birthday party that goes wrong
   (b) a dragon who never learned to fly
   (c) a young boy born on another planet comes to Earth for the first time
   (d) two friends have a fight over a competition

You may want to choose your favorite beginning and complete the story to share with the class.

STUDENT WRITING 13

Writing Dialogue

Put the missing capitals and punctuation marks in these sentences.

1. You'll just have to get used to it, she said crossly.

2. "Wow said Tracey. "You really snore loudly, Martine

3. Paula explained to Tracey "At the end of it all, the soggy rag will splosh right in Martine's face.

4. anyhow, I think I can— Bronwyn began to say

5. Do you think it will work tracey asked

Read the sentences below and find the one sentence that doesn't have any errors in capitalization or punctuation. Circle that sentence.

6. "It was so much fun filling everyone's shower cap with talcum powder!", exclaimed Lois.

7. Tracey said quietly. "Martine Kirby's father owns a chocolate factory."

8. Everyone was saying politely "Excuse me Martine, but do you think that you might . . ."

9. "I'll just have to invent a special machine that cures snoring," said Paula, who came from a long line of engineers.

10. I don't want to go home yet and miss camp," Bronwyn said.

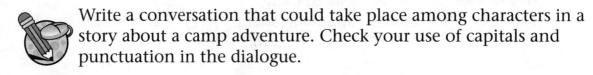 Write a conversation that could take place among characters in a story about a camp adventure. Check your use of capitals and punctuation in the dialogue.

Store your writing in your portfolio. You might want to write the complete story later.

COLLECTIONS 6 Copyright © 1999 Prentice Hall Ginn Canada.
Permission to reproduce this page is restricted to the purchasing school.

personal reading responses

Read the following narratives by yourself or with a friend. Jot your personal responses in each of the three areas. Examples are provided to help you get started. Discuss your responses with the class.

The Quilt

To me, a house is a warm and safe place. A house is welcoming and respectful at the same time. A house is strong and gentle and sensitive. That's why I picked a house for my square of the class quilt.

by Ruth Gallivan-Smith
from *And the Message Is...*

My Feelings	Some Comparisons	My Opinion
– the words made me feel good and warm inside –	– this house reminds me of my grandma's –	– I like some of the descriptive words, but I would have used some different words –

Animals

Animals. What would we do without them? Well, if we don't stop killing our animals, we'll soon find the answer to that question. I don't even want to think about a world without animals. Sure, you can kill the animals for necessary food, but don't just kill them for sport—that isn't fair. If you do, then our animals will be extinct. Anytime that you think that you need to kill an animal, remember this...

WHAT WOULD THE WORLD BE LIKE WITHOUT ANIMALS???

by Leanne Zucchero
from *Together Is Better*

My Feelings	Some Comparisons	My Opinion

Make A Dream Catcher (A)

What You Need:

- 1 ring, wooden hoop, or cut the outside rim of a large margarine lid
- 7 metres of yarn, string, or cord
- approximately 15 small beads for decoration
- feathers for decoration
- leather thongs, twine, shoelaces, or burlap rope

What You Do:

1. Glue yarn (or string or cord) onto the hoop. Wind yarn around to completely cover the hoop.

2. Using 4 metres of yarn, knot end onto hoop. Make a loop approximately 3.5 cm away from the first knot. Continue around the entire hoop. It helps if you keep the hoop lying on a flat surface as the loops are assembled.

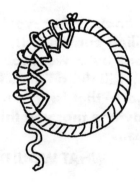

3. Bring yarn to the bottom of first loop and knot. Make loop to begin second round as shown. Continue all the way around.

Make A Dream Catcher (B)

4. Repeat Step 3 twice more, making the loops slightly smaller each time around. Weave end of yarn through the last round of loops. Pull tightened web, leaving a hole in the centre. Knot and trim the ends.

larkspur knot

5. Cut three 30 cm pieces of thong (or twine, shoelaces, or rope) and attach each one to the hoop using a larkspur knot. Decorate each thong with beads and feathers.

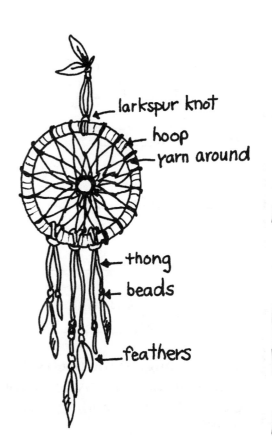

larkspur knot
hoop
yarn around
thong
beads
feathers

6. To finish, cut a small piece of yarn for a hanger, attach to the hoop using a larkspur knot, and add a bead and a feather.

Rhyming Words

Write two or three rhyming words for each of these words.

1. bright	2. mind	3. cloak
4. praise	5. glare	6. moon
7. sweep	8. town	9. snow

Choose four pairs of rhyming words, and for each pair, write a two line poem. For example:

glare and bare

The tree, with her snarled limbs shook bare,
Stooped sadly under the moon's icy glare.

10. ____and_____

11. _____and_____

12._____and_____

13.____and_____

Look through some poetry books to see how other writers use rhyming words in their poems. Find your favorite examples and share them with a classmate before adding them to your personal list for reference for future writing.

ous pattern; suffixes; irregular spellings

How Music Was Fetched Out of Heaven

unfriendliness	dangerously
contentment	siege
mountainous	readiness
fiery	column
nothingness	marvellous
generous	mightiest

unfriendliness
contentment
mountainous
fiery
nothingness
generous
dangerously
siege
readiness
column
marvellous
mightiest

affixes; al pattern

A Young Painter: The Life and Paintings of Wang Yani

unnecessary	essential
frequently	approval
unnatural	visually
personal	necessarily
independently	encouraging
concentrating	horizontal

unnecessary
frequently
unnatural
personal
independently
concentrating
essential
approval
visually
necessarily
encouraging
horizontal

2- and 3-syllable words; able pattern

Wildland Visions

unattainable		
reserve		
tribute		
camera		
reasonable		
supreme		
tropical		
unique		
splendor		
(splendour)		
default		
recognizable		
diesel		

unattainable	tropical
reserve	unique
tribute	splendor
camera	(splendour)
reasonable	default
supreme	recognizable
diesel	

-ed, -ity, -ly patterns

Fast Forward Art

published		
demonstrated		
normally		
wonderfully		
popularity		
modified		
inspired		
accurately		
originality		
especially		
quality		
reproduced		

published	inspired
demonstrated	accurately
normally	originality
wonderfully	especially
popularity	quality
modified	reproduced

Fax Facts

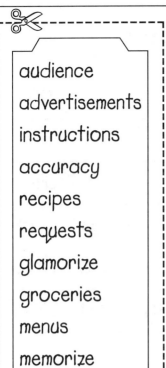

| audience | advertisements | instructions | accuracy | recipes | requests | glamorize | groceries | menus | memorize | service | mathematics |

audience	glamorize
advertisements	groceries
instructions	menus
accuracy	memorize
recipes	service
requests	mathematics

☐ plurals; soft "c" pattern; /īze/ sound

In Your Face

| facial | structure | features | electronics | criminal | physical | measurement | realistic | digital | future | creatures | specific |

facial	measurement
structure	realistic
features	digital
electronics	future
criminal	creatures
physical	specific

☐ ure, al, ic patterns

Anti-Snore Machine

generously	vigorous
previously	indignantly
tremendous	doubtfully
extremely	momentous
successfully	desperately
apologetically	sympathetically

generously
previously
tremendous
extremely
successfully
apologetically
vigorous
indignantly
doubtfully
momentous
desperately
sympathetically

Dancing the Cotton-Eyed Joe

intentional	contradict
behavior	signalling
admission	unintentional
behaving	complicate
uncomfortable	specialty
figuring	discomfort

intentional
behavior
admission
behaving
uncomfortable
figuring
contradict
signalling
unintentional
complicate
specialty
discomfort

Appendices

*A*ppendix 1
Index of Key Learning Expectations/Assessment

READING	Teaching Opportunities	Assessment Opportunities		
Overall Expectations	**TRM**	**TRM**	**LSC**	**AH**
• read a variety of fiction and non-fiction materials for different purposes	pp. 12, 19, 49, 62, 69, 77, 101, 131, 140	12, 19, 69 (BLM 10), 74, 77*, 101, 131, 140	45*	㉑ , ㉖
• read independently, selecting appropriate reading strategies	p. 55	55*		
• explain their interpretation of a written work, supporting it with evidence from the work and from their own knowledge and experience	pp. 19, 34, 40, 55, 70, 84, 92, 109, 116, 122, 137	34 (BLM 5), 38, 40, 55, 70, 84, 92*, 109 (BLM 17), 122 (BLM 19), 137		㉖
• understand the vocabulary and language structures appropriate for this grade level	pp. 93, 122			
Expectations in Specific Areas	**TRM**	**TRM**	**LSC**	**AH**
Reasoning and Critical Thinking • identify the elements of a story and explain how they relate to each other	p. 11	11		
• make predictions while reading a story or novel, using various clues	p. 108	108		
• summarize and explain the main ideas in information materials, and cite details that support the main ideas	pp. 25, 33, 49, 76, 85, 116	25 (BLM 4), 31, 33, 49 (BLM 9), 76, 85*, 89, 116		
• make judgements and draw conclusions about ideas in written materials on the basis of evidence	p. 26	26*		㉖
• identify a writer's perspective or character's motivation	pp. 41, 63	41*, 46		
Understanding of Form and Style • identify different forms of writing and describe their characteristics	p. 102	102*		
• use their knowledge of the characteristics of different forms of writing to select the appropriate materials for a specific purpose	p. 134	134		

Key:
* Model or Criteria for Checklist/Rubric   ◯Reading Passages Assessment Master
TRM = Teacher's Resource Module   LSC= Learning Strategy Card   AH = Assessment Handbook

WRITING

Overall Expectations	Teaching Opportunities TRM	Assessment Opportunities TRM	LSC	AH
• communicate ideas and information for a variety of purposes and to specific audiences	pp. 86, 117	117*, 120	47	
• use writing for various purposes and in a range of contexts, including school work	p. 47	47 (BLM 8)		
• use a variety of sentence types and sentence structures appropriate for their purposes	p. 110	114	50	
• produce pieces of writing using a variety of forms, techniques, and resources appropriate to the form and purpose, and materials from other media	pp. 12, 27, 42, 50, 102	12*, 27, 46, 50*, 102 (BLM 15), 106	39*	
• use correctly the conventions (spelling, grammar, punctuation, etc.) specified for this grade level	pp. 35, 70, 94, 123, 128	35 (BLM 6), 70 (BLM 11), 94 (BLM 14), 123, 128 (BLM 22)	41*, 49*	

Expectations in Specific Areas	TRM	TRM	LSC	AH
Word Use and Vocabulary Building • select words and expressions to create specific effects	pp. 20, 56, 64, 78, 90	20 (BLM 3), 23, 60, 90 (BLM 13)	44*	

ORAL AND VISUAL COMMUNICATION

Overall Expectations	TRM	TRM	LSC	AH
• make reports, describe and explain a course of action, and follow detailed instructions	p. 112			
• communicate a main idea about a topic and describe a sequence of events	pp. 79, 86	79 (BLM 12), 82, 86*	46, 48	

Expectations in Specific Areas	TRM	TRM	LSC	AH
Non-verbal Communication Skills • use tone of voice and gestures to enhance the message and help convince or persuade listeners in conversations, discussions, or presentations	pp. 72, 104, 124	72*, 104 (BLM 16), 124*, 127		
Group Skills • follow up on others' ideas, and recognize the validity of different points of view in group discussions or problem-solving activities	p. 64	64*, 67		
Media Communication Skills • analyze and assess a media work and express a considered viewpoint about it	pp. 14, 58, 118	16, 118		
• create a variety of media works	pp. 21, 29, 36, 44, 51, 97	36*, 44 (BLM 7), 53, 97*, 99	42*	

SELECTION	GENRE	LINK TO EXPERIENCE		READ AND RESPOND TO TEXT	REVISIT THE TEXT (Mini-Lessons)		
					Reading	Writing	Oral Communication
How Music Was Fetched Out of Heaven TRM pp. 10-17	myth retold	Discuss the Need for Music	Recall "How" Tales and Myths	STRATEGY: *Double Look* [Assessment] Reader Response	Classify Images [Assessment]	• Write a Message • Language Workshop — Spelling (-ous; suffixes; irregular spellings)	Choose Background Music [Assessment]
Creators TRM pp. 18-23	poems	Define Creativity	Write About Self-Expression	STRATEGY: *Visualize and Sketch* [Assessment] Reader Response	Compare Poems	Appreciate and Write Metaphors [Assessment]	
A Young Painter: The Life and Paintings of Wang Yani TRM pp. 24-31	biography	Talk About a Mentor	List Ways of Learning How	STRATEGY: *Follow Along* [Assessment] Reader Response	Categorize Details	• Write a "Parts of Speech" Poem [Assessment] • Language Workshop — Spelling (affixes; al)	
Carving a Totem Pole TRM pp. 32-38	procedural text	Brainstorm Facts About Totem Poles	Talk About a Group Project	STRATEGY: *Read and Paraphrase* [Assessment] Reader Response	Distinguish Between Main and Supporting Details [Assessment]	Language Workshop — Punctuation (apostrophes)	
Wildland Visions TRM pp. 39-46	photos/ commentary	Gather Books About Wildlands	Web Definitions of "Wildland" Words	STRATEGY: *Read, Pause, and Reflect* [Assessment] Reader Response [Assessment]	Understand Features of a Personal Photo Essay [Assessment]	• Write Commentaries for Photos [Assessment] • Language Workshop — Spelling (2-, 3-syllable words; -able)	
student writing Communicating/ Expressing Yourself Through the Arts TRM p. 47	personal narrative essay personal narrative					Language Workshop — Style (descriptive language and expression)	
Get Set for the Net! TRM pp. 48-53	non-fiction account	Talk About the Word "Net"	Write About a Way of Communicating	STRATEGY: *Follow Along* [Assessment] Reader Response	Connect Summarizing Statements and Details	Present Information in Various Formats	
Fast Forward Art TRM pp. 54-60	computer art with commentaries	List Ways of Creating Art Pieces	Talk About Computer Terms	STRATEGY: *Read and Connect* [Assessment] Reader Response	Make an Information Matrix	• Write an Introduction [Assessment] • Language Workshop — Spelling (-ed,-ity, -ly)	
World Shrinkers TRM pp. 61-67	article	Categorize Ways of Learning About People	Talk About E-mail Addresses	STRATEGY: *Double Look* Reader Response	Determine Questions and Answers	Create Images	Participate in an Editing Conference [Assessment]
Fax Facts TRM pp. 68-74	short story	Learn About the Fax Machine	Talk About Being Preoccupied	STRATEGY: *Follow Along* [Assessment] Reader Response	Read for the Moral or Lesson [Assessment]	• Language Workshop — Grammar (sentence fragments) • Language Workshop — Spelling (plurals; soft c; /ize/)	Read Orally with Expression
In Your Face TRM pp. 75-82	photo essay	Explore Distortions	Tell About Special Effect Distortions	STRATEGY: *Read and Summarize* [Assessment] Reader Response	Look at Unity and Coherence in a Paragraph	• Write Catchy Sentences • Language Workshop — Spelling (-ure, -al, -ic)	Give a Speech [Assessment]
Meet Emily of New Moon TRM pp. 83-89	interview	Talk About Famous Young People	Identify with a Movie/TV Character	STRATEGY: *Read and Connect* [Assessment] Reader Response [Assessment]	Categorize and Summarize Biographical Information	Write an Interview	Memorize Lines
student writing Communicating Through Mass Media TRM p. 90	limerick acrostic poem short story e-mail messages personal narrative					Language Workshop — Style (story openers) [Assessment]	
Anti-Snore Machine TRM pp. 91-99	short story	Illustrate Camp or Holiday Stories	Dramatize Snoring Situations	STRATEGY: *Read and Reflect* Reader Response	Explore Vocabulary	• Language Workshop — Punctuation (dialogue) • Language Workshop — Spelling (-ly, -ous)	
Listen with Your Eyes TRM pp. 100-106	article	List Ways to Get Messages from People	Act Out a Title	STRATEGY: *Read, Paraphrase, and Teach* Reader Response [Assessment]	Identify Ways of Providing Information	Language Workshop — Style (italics and quotation marks) [Assessment]	
Dancing the Cotton-Eyed Joe TRM pp. 107-114	short story	Talk About Dances and Dancing	Write About Making a Friend	STRATEGY: *Narrated Reading* [Assessment] Reader Response	Reading Between the Lines	•Write and Revise a Personal Narrative [Assessment] • Language Workshop — Spelling (words pairs; 3-syllable words)	Follow a Square Dance Call
All the Places to Love TRM pp. 115-120	picture book story	Draw a Special Place	List and Categorize Places	STRATEGY: *Listen and Read Along* [Assessment] Reader Response	Identify Story Themes	Write a Memory Poem [Assessment]	
Speak Your Dreams TRM pp. 121-127	poems	Talk About Personal Dreams	Brainstorm Descriptive Words	STRATEGY: *Listen and Sketch* Reader Response	Personalize a Reader Response	Discuss Hyphenated Words [Assessment]	Memorize a Poem for Presentation [Assessment]
student writing Communicating in Person TRM p. 128	poem report					Language Workshop — Style (rhyming words)	

Visual Communication	LINK TO CURRICULUM				LEARNING STRATEGY CARDS	BLACKLINE MASTERS
	Language Arts Write a "How" Story	Science • Find Out About Sound Waves • Research Alexander Graham Bell	The Arts Create a Picture Story	Social Studies Make an Ancient Mayan Question-and-Answer Book	#39 Purposes of Language	BLM 23: Spelling
Paint a Picture	Language Arts Read Poetry	Language Arts Investigate an Artist	The Arts Present Forms of Self-Expression	The Arts Illustrate Metaphors		BLM 3: Meeting Metaphors
Create a Picture from Memory	Language Arts Make a Poster	The Arts Draw a Picture from a Line	The Arts Use Music to Inspire a Painting	Social Studies Find Out About a Place in China	#40 Parts of Speech	BLM 4: Follow Along Grid (1) BLM 23: Spelling
Create a Model of a Totem Pole	Language Arts Write a News Report	Language Arts Tell a Story from Pictures	Social Studies Find Out More About Totem Poles	The Arts Arrange for a Speaker	#41 Apostrophes	BLM 5: Main and Supporting Details BLM 6: Work with Apostrophes
Develop Skills for Taking Photographs	Language Arts Write a Poem	The Arts Design a Logo	Social Studies • Make a Directory • Find Newspaper Clippings	Social Studies Make a Labelled Map	#42 Taking Photographs	BLM 7: Taking a Photograph BLM 24: Spelling
						BLM 8: Write with Description
Make a Flow Chart or Map Assessment	Language Arts Write a Script	Technology Conduct Research on the Internet	Technology Find Out About Early Computers	Social Studies • Learn About Earth Day • Research an Inventor	#43 Using a Search Engine	BLM 9: Follow Along Grid (2)
Compare Digital Art Pieces	Language Arts/Technology Write/Give Instructions	Language Arts/Technology Critique Computer Programs	The Arts Sponsor a Digital Art Display/Contest	Social Studies Learn About Digital Art in Movies	#44 Writing an Introductory Paragraph	BLM 24: Spelling
	Language Arts Write a Keypal or Penpal	Science Write an Animal Report Technology Explore Communication Technology	Social Studies Set Up an Information Corner	Social Studies Learn About Folk Festivals		
	Language Arts Write a Story with a Lesson	Language Arts/The Arts Draw a Cartoon Strip	The Arts Hold a Sing-ALong	Social Studies Discuss Interpersonal Relationships and Technology	#45 Self-Evaluation	BLM 10: Follow Along Grid (3) BLM 11: Sentence Fragments BLM 25: Spelling
	Language Arts Write a Limerick	Language Arts Play an Identification Game	The Arts Age or Morph a Character	Science Learn About the Face	#46 Speeches	BLM 12: Talk It Up BLM 25: Spelling
	Language Arts • Make a Book Collection • Create a Commercial	Language Arts/The Arts Compare a Book and Movie	Social Studies Learn About Prince Edward Island	Social Studies/Mathematics Create a Game	#47 Interviewing #48 Learning to Memorize	
						BLM 13: Interesting Ways to Begin
Create a Flow Diagram Assessment	Language Arts Write a Sequence Poem	Language Arts/The Arts Perform a Readers' Theatre	Health Find Out About Snoring	Science/Mathematics Find Out About Noise Levels	#49 Writing Dialogue	BLM 14: Writing Dialogue BLM 26: Spelling
Perform a Mime	Language Arts Write a One-Act Pantomime The Arts Listen to a Conductor	Social Studies Make a Cultural Gestures Book	Mathematics Create an Orbital Diagram	Science Learn About the Body Language of an Animal		BLM15: Uses of Italics and Quotation Marks BLM 16: Up a Rope
	Language Arts Read Stories About People with Disabilities	Science/Health Research Blindness	Mathematics Design a Budget	The Arts Learn a Dance	#50 Types of Sentences	BLM 17: Reading Between the Lines BLM 26: Spelling
Compare Illustration and Text Assessment	Language Arts • Find Similes • Play "Categories"	Language Arts/The Arts Illustrate a Cluster of Words	Language Arts/The Arts Design a Birth Announcement Card	Science Draw and Label Plants and Animals		BLM 18: Memory Poems
	Language Arts Audio Tape a Poem	Social Studies Discuss Solutions for Problems	Science Find Out About Dreams and Dreaming	The Arts Make a Dream Catcher		BLM 19: Personal Reading Responses BLMs 20 & 21: Make a Dream Catcher
						BLM 22: Rhyming Words

Appendix 3   Unit Spelling Words

HOW MUSIC WAS FETCHED OUT OF HEAVEN

• *ous pattern; suffixes; irregular spellings*

unfriendliness	contentment	mountainous
fiery	nothingness	generous
dangerously	siege	readiness
column	marvellous	mightiest

Theme/Challenge Words

• *music and world of the gods*

Quetzalcoatl	Tezcatlipoca	cadence
citadel	monumental	

Early Words

• *-le pattern*

tremble	grumble	circle
cable	miracle	

A YOUNG PAINTER: THE LIFE AND PAINTINGS OF WANG YANI

• *affixes; al pattern*

unnecessary	frequently
unnatural	personal
independently	concentrating
essential	approval
visually	necessarily
encouraging	horizontal

Theme/Challenge Words

• *people in the arts*

Beethoven	Schubert
Mozart	Wang Yani
Yikuo Hiyayama	

Early Words

• *1-syllable words*

strict	sense	
fruit	praise	solve

WILDLAND VISIONS

• *2- and 3-syllable words; able pattern*

unattainable	reserve	tribute
camera	reasonable	supreme
tropical	unique	diesel
default	splendor	(splendour)
recognizable		

Theme/Challenge Words

• *wildland words*

Bay du Nord	sponges
bounteous	bladderworts
ecological	

Early Words

• *double letters*

struggle	freedom
choose	occur
between	

FAST FORWARD ART

• *-ed, -ity, -ly patterns*

published	demonstrated
normally	wonderfully
popularity	modified
inspired	accurately
originality	especially
quality	reproduced

Theme/Challenge Words

• *Internet words*

protocol	modulator
modem	cyberspace
emoticon	

Early Words

• *er pattern*

modern	interesting
patterns	everyone
computer	

FAX FACTS

• *plurals; soft "c" pattern; /īze/ sound*

audience	advertisements
instructions	accuracy
recipes	requests
glamorize	groceries
menus	memorize
service	mathematics

Theme/Challenge Words

• *fax words*

document	facsimile
correspondence	electronically
transmission	

Early Words

• *past tense words*

pretended	worried
heard	wandered
reminded	

IN YOUR FACE

• *ure, al, ic patterns*

facial	structure	features
electronics	criminal	physical
measurement	realistic	digital
future	creatures	specific

Theme/Challenge Words

• *digital art words*

morphing	distortion
animators	warping
reconstruction	

Early Words

• *-ly pattern*

early	actually
quickly	probably
amazingly	

ANTI-SNORE MACHINE

• *ly, ous patterns*

generously	previously
tremendous	extremely
successfully	apologetically
vigorous	indignantly
doubtfully	momentous
desperately	sympathetically

Theme/Challenge Words

• *television words*

audition	commercials
episode	understudies
Seinfeld	

Early Words

• *y as a syllable*

greedy	ordinary
sticky	factory
weary	

DANCING THE COTTON-EYED JOE

• *word pairs; 3-syllable words*

intentional	behavior
admission	behaving
uncomfortable	figuring
contradict	signalling
unintentional	complicate
specialty	discomfort

Theme/Challenge Words

• *dance words*

country-western	polka
schottische	waltz
square-dancing	

Early Words

• */o͝u/ sound*

touches	young
couples	youngest
country	